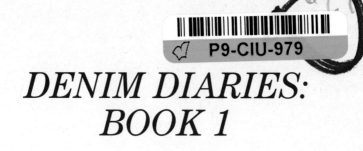

DENIM DIARIES: BOOK 1

SIXTEEN GOING ON TWENTY-ONE

DENIM DIARIES: BOOK 1

SIXTEEN GOING ON TWENTY-ONE

DARRIEN LEE

URBAN
Renaissance

www.urbanbooks.com

Urban Books
1199 Straight Path
West Babylon, NY 11704

Denim Diaries: Book One Sixteen Going On Twenty-One copyright
© 2009 Darrien Lee

ISBN- 13: 978-1-933967-71-4
ISBN- 10: 1-933967-71-4

First Printing January 2009
Printed in the United States of America

10   9   8   7   6   5   4

Distributed by Kensington Publishing Corp.
Submit Wholesale Orders to:
Kensington Publishing Corp.
C/O Penguin Group (USA) Inc.
Attention: Order Processing
405 Murray Hill Parkway
East Rutherford, NJ 07073-2316
Phone: 1-800-526-0275
Fax: 1-800-227-9604

DENIM DIARIES: BOOK 1

SIXTEEN GOING ON TWENTY-ONE

Prologue

"So, Denim, are you ready for our dance?"

Looking at her watch, Denim then looked up into Dré's handsome brown eyes and blushed. "Yes, but we have to make it fast because I have to get back home before my mom wakes up."

The DJ put on the slow song Dré requested and Dré quickly pulled Denim out onto the dance floor. Within seconds he had her in his arms, and it felt wonderful. As they danced to the rhythm of the song, Denim peered over Dré's shoulder and could tell that most of the girls in the room were envious of her. She pressed her face against his warm neck and let out a breath. Dré was making her feel things she'd heard about but never experienced before. She felt an unfamiliar sensation in her stomach and was totally lost in the moment.

Once the song ended, Dré continued to hold Denim in

his arms. Their hearts were beating wildly in their chests as they stared into each other's eyes. Just as another slow song began and she cuddled into Dré's arms once more, she was brought back to reality by a loud, popping noise. Seconds later, someone screamed.

"He's got a gun!"

Everyone panicked and started running toward the exit in what seemed like slow motion. It was total chaos as more than a hundred people ran for the front door. Dré held Denim close as they crouched low to the floor.

"Stay close to me, Denim!"

Tears were already streaming down her face. "What's going on, Dré?"

"Someone's shooting. Stay down!"

It was dark inside the room, but Dré noticed another exit in the opposite direction from where the crowd was going. As they started to run, Denim tripped over something, which caused her to slip and fall. Dré quickly helped her up and they continued out the other door and down the street. Denim lost both of her shoes, but still managed to run stride for stride with Dré. In the distance, they could hear the sounds of sirens approaching the recreation center. Denim could also feel her heart beating through her chest, and there was a sharp pain in her shoulder. Sweat was pouring down her face and back as she slowed her pace.

"Dré, wait! I can't go any farther!"

"Yes, you can! I have to get you home!"

Crying, Denim begged him to stop. "Please, Dré, I can't run any more."

Stopping briefly, he leaned over to catch his breath. As the pair stood there gasping for air, Denim frantically questioned him.

"What happened back there?"

"I'm not sure, but it sounded like someone shooting."

"Shooting? Why would someone be shooting at your party?" she asked.

He looked over at Denim and fear immediately gripped his body. "Denim! Oh my God! Look at your blouse!"

She looked down and nearly fainted. Her blouse was stained with a red substance that appeared to be blood. Dré quickly grabbed her in a panic and ripped open her blouse.

"Are you hit?" He ran his hands over her soft skin, looking for anything that could be a bullet wound.

"I'm so sorry, Denim," he whispered with tears in his eyes.

If only Denim had listened to her mother, none of this would be happening to her right now. It was all like a dream, and her life was spiraling out of control. If only she could turn back the hands of time and do things differently. Or could she?

Chapter One

*E*arlier that day, Denim entered her bedroom, slamming the door behind her. She couldn't believe her mom wouldn't let her go to Dré's house party. She was going to be sixteen in two months, and her mom promised her she would start giving her more freedom.

Denim shared a home with her mom, Valessa, and dad, Samuel, in Freedman, California. Her oldest brother, Antoine, was a sophomore at Morehouse College in Atlanta, Georgia.

The door swung open and Valessa entered angrily.

"Denim, if you slam another door in this house, you won't see the light of day until you're twenty-one! Do you understand me?"

"Yes, ma'am," she answered, lowering her head. "But Mom, I don't understand why you won't let me go to Dré's party. It's a teen party and everybody's going to be there but me."

"That's what *you* say. I don't trust Dré's parents. They're young and seem very irresponsible to me. Besides, I've been hearing rumors about Dré, and I don't want you associated with him."

"What kind of rumors, Mom?" Denim asked curiously.

Folding her arms, Valessa sighed. "I heard that Dré smokes marijuana."

Looking away, Denim played with the large, white teddy bear on her bed. "I wouldn't know anything about that, Mom."

Turning to walk out of the room, Valessa rolled her eyes. "Sure you wouldn't. You teenagers know everything about each other. I wasn't born yesterday, Denim. Stay away from him, and I mean it!"

"But Mom!"

"Denim, if you 'but Mom' me one more time!"

Denim threw herself on the bed in frustration as her mother leaned against the doorframe in silence. Yes, Denim had heard the rumors about Dré, but she'd never witnessed him smoking, so how was she to know whether it was true?

Dré was the most popular guy in school, and every girl was after him. Dré and Denim had been emailing each other for some time now, and as each email arrived from him, he revealed more and more about his feelings for her. Just the thought of him sent shivers over her body, but she couldn't let her mother know what effect Dré had upon her. Bottom line was that Dré was the only man she wanted to go out with. She just hoped he wasn't playing her and that she was the only girl he wanted as well.

Unfortunately, getting her parents to understand was another story, and Denim knew that her parents wouldn't approve of her dating Dré.

Valessa remembered that Dré's parents were barely into their thirties. His dad owned a questionable business selling used cars. Their lifestyle was always under suspicion, not only by Valessa and Samuel, but by others in the neighborhood as well. Most believed that the business was being used as a front for something more sinister.

Valessa walked over to Denim's bed and sat down next to her. She took a breath and spoke calmly. "They're just too out there for me, Denim. I'm afraid something might happen to you. Can't you understand that? I love you, and you're my only daughter. If I let you go to this party, I would never forgive myself if you got hurt or killed. Now, that's enough about Dré's party. Why don't you call Patrice to come over?"

Patrice was Denim's best friend and partner in crime. They'd been friends since third grade, when Patrice's family moved to Freedman by way of New Orleans. She had that Cajun accent that made it hard for people to understand her at times. But Denim could understand every word she said. Patrice was loud, always happy and ready to party, and extremely boy-crazy.

"Patrice is going to the party," she mumbled while hugging her stuffed teddy bear.

"I'm sorry, but there's nothing I can do about that. You're my responsibility, not Patrice."

Denim rolled over on the bed and sat up next to her mother.

"It's not fair. You and Daddy let Antoine do a lot more than you're letting me."

"Denim, you're probably right, but this has nothing to do with your brother. Besides, he matured quicker than most sixteen-year-old boys, so we were able to give him a little more freedom earlier. I'm sorry, sweetheart, but I have a bad feeling about this party, and I will not change my mind. Look, why don't you come back into the family room and watch a movie with me?"

Denim rolled back over on the bed and hugged her teddy bear once again. "I don't feel like watching a movie."

"Okay, but if you change your mind, you're welcome to join me," Valessa said as she stood. "Oh! Don't forget your dad will be back tomorrow afternoon from his conference, so it would be a good idea if you straightened up the garage before he got back."

"Yes, ma'am," Denim whispered through sniffles.

Denim scooted off the bed and followed her mom out of the room and into the garage to begin her task.

Chapter Two

An hour or so later, Denim had the garage partially cleaned. As she carted the trash to the curb, she noticed a familiar physique strolling her way. She quickly knocked the dust off her pants and T-shirt. After running her hand quickly through her hair, she glanced over her shoulder to see if her mom was watching from the window. Thankfully, the coast was clear.

André Patterson, better known as Dré, had lived five houses down from Denim ever since they were three years old. He was a basketball star and budding artist, producing many sketches and painting for friends, as well as a mural at school. The two had been friends for a long time, but it wasn't until last year that Dré started looking differently. Instead of being the awkward, skinny kid he'd always been, he now had muscles bulging from everywhere, and a smile that lit up the sky. He was gorgeous! At six feet, he already had a body that made the girls swoon.

He was dressed in a pair of baggy jeans and a wife-beater tank top, which revealed his fabulous muscles. His hair was wavy and he wore it cut low. His cocoa brown skin was as smooth as a newborn's, and thick lashes framed a pair of light brown eyes with specks of green. When he smiled, two large dimples greeted Denim. He was just as handsome as his older brother, Savion, who was away in the Air Force.

"Hey, Dré! Where are you headed?" she asked with a bright smile.

"I thought I would stop by to see what you were wearing to my party tonight."

Sighing, she put the top on the garbage can and looked away briefly.

"I won't be able to come to your party, Dré. As you can see, my mom has me pretty busy."

He smiled, and her heart melted. Dré folded his arms and stared directly at her.

"Your parents won't let you come, will they?"

Surprised by his ability to read her so well, she replied honestly. "Nah, they won't. They're sticking to their rules about me not going out until I'm sixteen. I'm sorry, Dré."

He reached over, took her hand into his, and caressed her knuckles. "Are you sure it's not because it's *my party*?" he asked.

Denim looked away, giving Dré his answer. He smiled

and said, "Don't sweat it, Denim. There'll be other parties, and your birthday's only a couple of months away. But I'm not going to lie and say I'm not disappointed. I was really hoping to dance with you tonight."

Denim's face became enflamed, and she prayed he didn't notice the change in her complexion as he continued to caress her hand. She blushed and tried to pull her hand away, but he held onto it.

"Like I said, I'm sorry. Besides, I'm sure Anika and those other girls will keep you busy on the dance floor." She pulled her hand away from his.

He leaned in and whispered into her ear. "Just so you know, I don't care about Anika or any of those other girls, so I won't be slow dancing with anyone, since you won't be there."

She looked into his beautiful brown eyes and smiled. "You don't have to do that, Dré."

He took a step away from her and laughed out loud. "I know, but I don't want to slow dance with anyone else. You know you're the only girl for me, even if you are sweaty and covered in dust."

Denim giggled as she looked down at her T-shirt.

"Seriously, Denim, there is no one else, so I guess you're going to have to get used to it, huh?"

"R-R-Really?" she stuttered, stunned by Dré's admission. "I mean, I know you said in your email that you thought I was special, but I didn't know you wanted me to be your girl."

He leaned toward her quickly and kissed her on the cheek. "Well, now you know."

"Are you sure?" she asked, still somewhat dumb-founded

"No doubt!" he replied out loud as he mimicked shooting a basketball.

"I'd like that."

"Good," he answered.

She looked down at the ground and hesitated for moment. When she looked up, Dré could tell something was bothering her.

"Can I ask you something?"

"Sure," he answered as he tossed a rock down the street.

"Are you messing around with drugs?"

He put his hands in his pockets. "I smoke a little weed sometimes. Why?"

Disappointed, she shook her head in disbelief. Even though she wanted an honest man, she was praying he would deny it or at least lie to cover his tracks.

"People talk and it's gotten back to my parents. And just so you know, drugs are not my thang, and they shouldn't be yours either."

Dré lowered his head for a moment and then gazed into her eyes. "Look, Denim, I have one mother. I don't need another one. You feel me?"

She kicked the garbage can in anger. "Whatever, Dré. I'm just telling you!" she yelled as she started to walk away.

Her reaction got his attention, and he realized just how upset she was with him. He ran after her and grabbed her arm.

"Why are you trippin'? It's just a little weed."

"Why?" she asked. "Dré, I like you, but I won't go out with you if you're taking drugs, and there's no such thing as *just a little weed.*"

"Do you love me?"

Startled, her head snapped around toward him. "What did you say?"

"Do you love me?" he asked again.

She knew immediately that this wasn't a joke because his eyes were glazed and his voice was cracking. His question caught her off guard, making her a little nervous.

"I shouldn't have to answer that, Dré."

"And I shouldn't have to ask it either, Denim."

"Then why are you asking me?"

"Because I need to know."

"It doesn't matter because if you're doing drugs, we are over before we start."

They were going toe-to-toe, and Denim knew she wasn't tough enough to go up against him. She was weak around him, always had been, and she also knew she'd loved him since they were in kindergarten.

"This is crazy," he mumbled as he turned away from her.

She grabbed his arm and turned him around to face her. "Why does it have to be crazy? You're an athlete, Dré, and drugs are not good for your health. You could get into some serious trouble if you're ever caught with that stuff."

He stared at her. "Forget all that. You didn't answer my question of whether you love me or not."

She put her hands on her hips. "And I'm not going to, either, because I didn't think you had to ask me to know the answer. We go way back, Dré."

Dré released her and sat down on the curb to wipe the dust off his leather Jordans. "I know, Denim. You've always been my girl, even in kindergarten, but I need to hear it." Dré had no idea what had come over him. For some reason, he wanted to see if she would confirm her feelings for him.

Denim put her hands on her hips and stared down at him. Both were silent for a few minutes before she sat down beside him.

"I want something from you too," she admitted.

He looked over at her and asked, "What?"

"Are you going to leave that stuff alone?"

Without looking up at her, he replied, "I know what I'm doing, Denim, so don't worry. A'ight?"

"That's not what I asked you."

Agitated, he looked over at her and said, "Oh, I have to answer your question, but you can't answer mine?"

Denim linked her arm with his and whispered, "The drugs are the reason Mom and Dad don't want me hanging out with you, so I need to know if you'll give it up."

He turned to face her again and noticed tears in her eyes.

"I smoke a little from time to time. It's harmless, Denim! I know your mom and dad think I'm a thug, but if it takes giving up weed to be with you, I'll do it."

She tilted her head and studied his facial expression.

"Do you promise?"

He reached over and gently wiped a smudge of dirt off her cheek."I promise."

Denim smiled and kissed him on the cheek."Thank you, Dré."

"You're welcome. Now, back to you. Do you love me?"

She laid her head on his shoulder and softly replied, "Yes."

Dré briefly closed his eyes and smiled. He leaned over and kissed her forehead before standing. "Perfect. Look, I'll holler at you later."

Denim stood and pulled her hair up into a ponytail. "Have fun at your party tonight."

He started walking slowly down the street, and then turned back to her. "I doubt it since you're not going to be there. Later, Denim."

"Bye, Dré."

Denim hoped her comments hadn't pushed Dré away because she really did care deeply for him. More truthfully, she loved him and always had. If he ruined his life over something stupid like drugs, she would never forgive him.

She turned and slowly walked back into the garage to finish cleaning. What she didn't know was that her mom had watched the entire scene from the kitchen window. It was then that Valessa Mitchell realized Denim was growing up. She wasn't her baby girl anymore, and she would have to treat her like a young woman.

* * *

As Dré walked down the block, he recalled how it felt to hear Denim ask him about the drugs. It caught him off guard, and it bothered him to know she disapproved. He had been around weed most of his life, and unfortunately, it was a normal fixture to him. He'd seen his parents smoking most of his young years, and now it had become his bad habit.

He jumped the rock wall in front of his house and walked around to the backyard. He found a seat on a large tree trunk, reached into his pocket, and pulled out a joint. Lighting it, he inhaled and thought about the day when he would get out of Freedman and hopefully take Denim with him. But for now, he would have to walk softly around her parents until he figured out a way to get them to trust him with their daughter.

An hour later the garage was clean, so Denim ate a quick dinner, showered, and dressed for bed. She turned on her stereo and popped in a Keyshia Cole CD she had purchased earlier that week. Climbing onto the bed, she pulled out her prized possession, a journal that her grandmother gave her for her thirteenth birthday. This was the place she wrote her most personal thoughts. Keeping a journal had become a popular trend among girls her age.

Denim moved all her stuffed animals off her bed and pulled back her comforter. She fluffed her pillows, climbed into bed, picked up her pen, and started writing:

Today wasn't a good day. I got into a big argument with Mom because she told me I couldn't go to Dré's party. She's trippin' because of the rumors she heard about him and drugs. Even though the rumors are true, she's known Dré all his life. I wish Daddy were here because I know he would probably let me go to the party.

Oh! I almost forgot . . . Dré came over and out of the blue he wanted to know if I loved him. Well, I didn't know what to say at first, even though I knew the answer. I just didn't know if I wanted him to know my answer. Anyway, I finally caved and told him the truth . . . YES! I also told him he'd better leave that mess he's fooling around with alone. He tried to act like it wasn't serious, but I'm no fool.

I know if Mom knew Dré admitted to me that he got high, she would go ballistic. Anyway, I'll be sixteen soon and hopefully Mom will let me have a Sweet Sixteen party so I can dance with Dré all night long. Until next time.

Peace Out!
D

Closing her journal, she lay down and stared at the ceiling fan above her head. The music coming from her stereo relaxed her and was putting her to sleep. She was upset because she knew everyone was having fun down at the rec center. That was, everyone but her.

Just then, her mom knocked on the door.

"Denim?" her mother called out to her from outside the door.

Denim sat up to greet her mother. "You can come in."

Valessa opened the door and walked into the room. She sat down on the futon that housed Denim's stuffed animals. "Are you turning in?"

Denim leaned over and set her journal on the night-stand. "Since I don't have anything else to do, I might as well."

Valessa pointed her finger at Denim. "Watch your tone with me, young lady, or you'll miss every party this year."

Sitting up on her knees, Denim apologized. "I'm sorry."

"You'd better be. Denim, don't make me out to be the bad guy here. If I don't feel comfortable with Dré's party or any other party, you're not going, and that's the end of it."

Valessa stood and smoothed out the leg on her pink satin pajamas.

"I love you, Denim, and I hope you understand that I'm only trying to protect you. Now give me a good night hug."

Denim hugged her mother and kissed her good night. Within an hour, she was asleep.

Chapter Three

Time seemed to pass by quickly. An hour or so later, Denim was in a deep sleep when she was awakened by an unknown noise. When she sat up, she heard it again. It sounded like tapping, but from where?

There it is again. What is that noise?

The only light in her room was from her stereo. She looked at the time on her clock, which read eleven-thirty. Climbing out of bed, she heard the noise once more, but this time at her window. Taking a deep breath, she tiptoed over to the window and nervously peeped out. She couldn't believe her eyes.

It's Dré!

Quietly raising her window, she stuck her head outside into the cool night air.

"Are you crazy?" she whispered. "What are you doing here?"

"I came to get you," he announced with a big grin on his face.

He was standing there wearing a brand new pair of jeans and a red button-down dress shirt. She could also tell that the pair of athletic footwear on his feet was new.

"My party is busted without you there," he whispered.

"Really?"

"Yes, really."

"I already told you I couldn't go, Dré."

He positioned his hands as if he were praying.

"Come on, Denim. Just one dance . . . please? I'll have you back before your mom even notices you're missing."

"You don't know her. She'll kill me, and when my dad comes home, he'll dig me up and kill me again."

She could see his thick lashes even in the moonlight. She would have to be crazy to go along with him. But her clothes were already picked out, so what harm could one dance do?

"Come on, girl!" he pleaded.

"Okay," she whispered, giving it one last thought, "but you're going to have to help me down from this window."

"Cool!" he said, grinning. "I got you, babe. Now hurry up."

Denim nervously dressed and sprayed perfume on her skin and rinsed her mouth out with mouthwash.

She had on some black capris and a yellow blouse. She tossed her black sandals out the window to Dré. To get out her window and climb down the side of her house, she put on a pair of athletic shoes. As she climbed down the trellis, she anticipated feeling Dré's hands on her body. Within minutes, she was in his arms, facing him.

He towered over her, smiling. "Thanks for coming. Dang! You smell great!"

"Thank you," she replied, blushing. "You have my shoes, right?"

He pointed to the ground, but before she could stoop to retrieve them, he leaned in to kiss her softly on the lips. Surprised, she stepped back from him and frowned.

"You've been smoking weed, haven't you?"

"Just a little," he answered with a goofy smile.

She squatted down to put on her shoes. "I told you I don't like that, and you promised me you'd quit."

"My bad," he said as he checked his breath. "It's my birthday, but I promise, after tonight, I'm giving it up for good."

Hiding her tennis shoes in the bushes, she turned to him. "You'd better, and if you break your promise again, it's over between us."

Dré could see the angry scowl on Denim's face in the moonlight, and he finally understood she really wasn't kidding. Not that he thought she was joking in the first place.

"I'm sorry, and I promise on the real this time. I don't want to lose you over something stupid like weed."

"Good. Look, I'll go to your party with you, but one dance, Okay?"

"Okay, but if I can get two dances with you, I'll definitely take it."

She turned her nose up at him. "Not if you keep smoking that stuff. It stinks and it makes you act different." She reached inside her pocket and opened a container of breath mints. "Open your mouth," she commanded.

When he complied, Denim popped two breath mints into his mouth and slid the container back inside her pocket.

"Thank you," he said as he put his arm around her shoulder.

He realized everything she was saying was true, and he would have to change his ways.

As they walked toward the recreation center, Denim felt nervous because she knew if her parents ever found out that she sneaked out of the house, she would be punished forever.

Back at the Mitchell house, Valessa tossed and turned in her sleep. She never was able to get a good night's sleep when her husband was out of town, and tonight would be no different.

Denim and Dré walked into the rec center together. All eyes were on them as they walked across the room and over to the refreshment table. Patrice ran up to Denim and pulled her to the side.

"Girl, I didn't think you were coming."

"Shhh, Patrice! I'm not supposed to be here. Dré came and got me, I climbed out my window so I could have one dance with him."

"Wow, Denim! I know your parents don't play, and if your mom finds out, you're dead."

Even though the music was loud, Denim motioned for Patrice to lower her voice.

"I know, Patrice. Now keep that on the down low."

"I will. Now go on and get your dance on because Dré's got his eye on you, girl!"

"See you later, Patrice."

"Have fun!" Patrice yelled.

Dré's eyes were on Denim as she made her way back over to him. His eyes revealed things that excited her and made her nervous.

He leaned down close to her ear.

"Are you ready for our dance?" he asked.

Denim glanced at her watch and felt weird. She felt as if something big was about to happen, but she didn't know what. Was it a premonition? Whatever it was, it wasn't a good feeling.

"Yes, but we have to make it fast because I have to get back home."

And that's when gunshots rang out and everyone scattered. After Denim fell, Dré and Denim made it outside and ran for safety.

"What happened?" Denim asked after she finally got Dré to stop running.

"I'm not sure, but I think someone started shooting. Denim! Oh my God! Look at your blouse!"

She looked down and nearly fainted. Her blouse was stained with a sticky red substance that appeared to be blood. Dré quickly grabbed her in a panic and ripped open her blouse.

"Are you hit?" He ran his hands over her soft skin. With fear in his heart, he unsnapped her bloodstained bra and lowered it for his eyes only. Denim was in too much shock to care about his eyes on her.

After he was sure she wasn't shot, he held her tightly. It was obvious how close the bullets were to them. It was then that he realized that Denim must have tripped near the person who got shot.

"I want to go home, Dré," Denim pleaded.

He removed his shirt and handed it to Denim to put on, and he tossed her bloodstained blouse and bra into a nearby dumpster. Standing there in only a white T-shirt, he apologized to her.

"I'm sorry, Denim. Let me get you home before your mom wakes up."

Holding her hand, they crossed several streets and tried their best to stay out of sight as they made their way back Denim's house. They continued to hear sirens in the distance as well as neighborhoods dogs barking, which made the whole scene feel eerie. Dré's cell phone rang, startling both of them. They stopped for a second so he could answer it.

"Yeah."

Denim watched Dré's facial expression as he listened to the caller.

"Yeah, I'm okay. Where are you guys?"

The suspense was killing Denim, and she couldn't wait until he got off the telephone.

"I don't know, Daddy. Who got shot?"

Denim tried to calm herself as she waited. Panicking wasn't something she needed to do right now.

"Nah, I don't know why he was there. He wasn't invited."

Dré's conversation seemed to be going from bad to worse.

"A'ight, Dad. I'm headed home."

He tucked the phone in his pocket, pulled two joints out of another pocket, and broke them up into tiny pieces and dropped them on the ground.

"That was my dad. He said they're okay, but the cops are all over the place. They told me to go on home."

"Who got shot?" she asked as she wiped her tears.

"This guy named Li'l Carl. He had no business at my party."

As they approached her house, she stifled her tears.

"Is he dead?"

"I don't know," he whispered. "Now be quiet so I can help you back into your window."

Dré climbed up on the trellis with Denim closely behind him. When he got to the top he slowly raised the window and climbed inside. He reached down and pulled Denim inside the room. She shivered as she stood there in shock. He couldn't take his eyes off her because if he hadn't been so selfish, they never would've been in this situation. Dré loved Denim, and he had almost cost her her life.

He noticed her robe on the bed, so he picked it up and wrapped it around her shoulders.

"You're shivering."

"I can't help it."

He held her in his arms and caressed her back. "I'm so sorry, Denim."

She stepped out of his embrace, causing the robe to fall to the floor. She removed Dré's shirt and quickly put on her robe. He put his shirt back on and hugged her once again.

"I'd better go. Denim, I had no idea . . ."

"I know, Dré," she whispered as she held onto him tightly. "It's not your fault. I'm so scared right now that I can't stop trembling. Thanks for saving me tonight."

He kissed her forehead.

"I think we saved each other, and I would never let anything happen to you."

She kissed him on his beautiful lips as tears slid down her cheeks.

"Please don't cry, Denim. You're safe now."

"I can't help it. My mom and dad will kill me if they find out what happened, and that I was there."

"Well, don't worry because my folks will be cool. They won't mention anything about you being there."

She released him and wiped the tears away with her hands.

"Thanks, Dré. Please be careful going home. Text me when you get home, okay?"

"I will. Bye," he said as he climbed out of her window.

And in that instant, he was gone. She quickly removed the rest of her clothes and climbed into bed. Before closing her eyes, she pulled out her journal and made a footnote to her previous entry.

> *P.S.*
> *Tonight I saw my life flash right before my eyes. There was drama beyond my wildest imagination, but Dré was my hero, and I'll never forget it. I love him so much.*

Closing her journal, she said a very special prayer, a prayer that Dré had his own awakening tonight. Clinging to her pillow, she forced herself to sleep, but she knew sleep wouldn't come easy.

Chapter Four

Getting ready for church the next morning wasn't very easy for Denim. She never did fall asleep the previous night, no matter how hard she tried. Getting Dré's text message after he got home should've put her at ease, but it didn't.

"Denim! Hurry up so you can eat breakfast!" her mother called from the kitchen.

"Okay!" Denim yelled as she checked her appearance in the mirror once more. Denim's eyes were bloodshot and her head was throbbing.

She'd tried on four outfits before she settled on a beige suit. As she hurried out of her bedroom, she nearly bumped into her mother in the hallway. Their eyes met and Valessa cupped Denim's face to inspect her more closely.

"Denim, you look terrible! Are you feeling okay?"

"I'm just tired," she answered as she looked away.

Valessa felt Denim's forehead and looked at her curiously.

"I don't know, Denim. You don't have a fever, but you look drained. Did you get enough sleep last night?"

"Not really, but I'll be okay."

"Is there anything you want to talk about, sweetie?" Valessa asked as she cupped her daughter's chin.

"No, ma'am," Denim answered as she walked past her mother.

"Well, when we get in from church, I want you to lie down," Valessa said, turning to follow Denim. "I can't have you looking pitiful when your daddy gets home."

"I'm okay, really, Mom."

"It's not up for discussion, Denim."

Denim sat down at the kitchen table and took a sip of orange juice. "Yes, ma'am."

Valessa put her empty coffee cup in the sink. "You weren't up all night chatting on your computer, were you?"

"No, ma'am."

Valessa couldn't put her finger on it, but she knew something was bothering Denim. She would have to deal with that later, though, because they were running late.

"Well, hurry up and eat your breakfast so we won't be late."

"I will."

Church service was longer than usual, and Denim did her best to stay awake. All she wanted to do was go home and go back to bed. She also wanted to talk to Dré to get more information about the shooting.

When church was finally over, Denim and her mother hurried to the car and climbed inside. Valessa turned up the air conditioner.

"I can't believe how hot it is so early in the morning. Take off your jacket, so you can cool off. My blouse is sticking to me."

Denim slid out of her jacket and placed it on the back seat. She lay back against the headrest in silence and let the cool air of the air conditioner soothe her body. Before pulling out of the church parking lot, Valessa adjusted her rearview mirror.

"Denim, Sister Vera said she heard that some child got shot down at the recreation center last night. Wasn't that the location where Dré was having his birthday party?"

Denim's eyes popped open in shock and she hesitated before answering.

"Yes, ma'am."

"See, that's why I didn't want you to go to that party. You just never know who's going to show up. Did any of your friends know anything about it?"

"No . . . well . . . I don't know. No one really talked about it."

Valessa looked over at her daughter, who was now staring out the passenger side window.

"Denim? Is there something going on that I should know about?"

Leave it alone already! Denim screamed inside her head.

Turning with a fake smile on her face, she answered. "No, ma'am. I just want to get home so I can take a nap. I'm starting to get a headache."

"Okay, but if there's something you want to talk about, I'm here."

"I know. Thanks."

Dré never got up this early on Sunday mornings. As he sat out on the brick wall in front of his house, he worked on a sketch he had started late last night. His best friend, DeMario, pulled up in front of the house and climbed out of his Toyota Camry. He shook hands with Dré and joined him on the wall.

"Hey, man, what's up?" DeMario greeted.

Without looking up from his sketch, Dré answered. "Nothing much, just trying to finish this sketch. What got you out so early?"

"My mom woke me up to go to the store for her," De-Mario said as he cleaned off his sunglasses. "I was sleeping good, too."

"I'm glad you were able to sleep. I've been up all night."

"I bet. Have you heard anything about what happened last night?"

Dré sighed and stopped sketching for a second. "Not really."

DeMario threw a rock at a cat crossing the street.

"Man, I ran like hell when I heard those gunshots. At first I thought it was firecrackers, but then I saw dude on the floor."

Dré started sketching again. "I grabbed Denim and got the hell out of there. She was so scared."

"I heard his name is Li'l Carl. Do you know him?" De-Mario asked.

Dré stopped drawing for a moment and shook his head. "I know of him. I heard he might have come up there with Stretch."

"Those guys are bad news everywhere they go. I usually leave the area when I see him coming because you know something's going to jump off. I won't be a bit surprised if he's involved some kind of way."

Dré stood up and wiped the sweat away from his forehead. "Well, none of them were invited, so they had no business there. My dad is pissed off that they brought some attention to him. He said he might catch a lot of heat because of it, too."

As a car slowly drove by, DeMario cautiously watched it. "Hopefully things will cool off quickly. Hey, Dré, that looks like Stretch's car."

Dré also watched the car as it drove by his house. "Nah, that's not him. He has tinted windows and spinners on the tires, remember?"

DeMario nodded in agreement. "Yeah, you're right, but it's the same color."

The pair watched as the car disappeared around the corner. "My dad said we have to be extra careful because somebody told him that five-O had been watching the house even before the shooting. My mom said she heard that dude lost a lot of blood and he's in a coma. He also might be paralyzed."

"That's messed up, Dré! Hey, you got a joint on you?"

"Nah," he answered, looking up from his canvas. "I'm thinking about giving that stuff up."

DeMario was waiting for the punch line to Dré's joke, but it never came.

"Wait, you don't have a joint, and you're giving it up?"

"You heard me," Dré responded.

DeMario was clearly surprised by Dré's announcement.

"I was going to see if you wanted to try this Ecstasy I picked up. I heard it was da bomb!"

Dré frowned. "Man, I'm definitely not fooling with any of that stuff. I have to think about my basketball career. My goal is to make it into the NBA. I won't be able to do that if I'm high all the time."

"So you're done with everything?" DeMario asked, shocked.

"Yeah, I'm done, and you need to leave it alone too," Dré said calmly. "I didn't think that much about it until I saw the look on Denim's face when I admitted to her that I got high."

DeMario smiled. "So you're quitting because of Denim, huh?"

"She has a lot to do with it. Everything she said was right, and I can't front like it's not."

DeMario slid the Ecstasy back inside his pocket.

"What are you drawing?"

"My girl."

"Who? Denim?"

"Yeah," Dré replied with a smile on his face.

DeMario stood and leaned against his car. He tugged on his jeans, which were two sizes too big. "I should've known. Have you talked to her today?"

"Nah, she's probably at church. I sent her a text when I got home last night."

"You're really into her, huh?"

"I've always been into her; you know that. But her mom and dad heard I got high, so they don't want me kicking it with her."

"That's messed up."

Setting his pencil down, Dré sighed. "I know, but I understand where they're coming from. I know I wouldn't want my daughter hanging out with some guy who got high. Would you?"

DeMario thought for a moment. "I see you've really given this a lot of thought since you're talking about kids and everything."

Looking toward Denim's house, Dré shrugged in silence. "It's the right thing to do."

"Have y'all done anything yet?"

Dré looked at DeMario with a smirk on his face.

"Denim's cool. Besides, I wouldn't step to her like that—at least not right now."

"You're a better man than I am," DeMario commented while shaking his head. "Denim has really filled out nicely this year. She's fine as hell, and all the brothas have been talking about her."

This bit of information caused Dré to stop sketching altogether. "Like who?"

"Everybody, Dré!"

"Well, they'd better stay away from her, because she's mine."

"Does Denim know that?" DeMario teased.

"Yeah, she knows," Dré said as he looked at his watch. "Look, I have to go."

DeMario opened his car door and climbed in. "Okay. I'll holler at you later."

Dré walked across the yard toward his house. He stepped onto the porch and then turned to DeMario. "Make sure you spread the word that Denim belongs to me."

Laughing, DeMario threw up his hand and waved good-bye. "Later!"

Chapter Five

The telephone rang, waking Denim out of her nap. She turned over, still exhausted from being awake all night. Lying there, she thought about Dré. Her mother peeped in the door with the telephone in her hand.

"Denim, your brother's on the telephone."

Denim sat up with excitement. She missed her brother and looked forward to talking to him every chance she got. Valessa handed her the telephone.

"Your dad just called," Valessa said before she exited the room. "He's stuck in traffic but should be home in about thirty minutes."

"Thanks."

Valessa closed the door as she heard Denim greet her brother.

"Hey, Antoine! What's going on?"

"Nothing much, little sis. What's happening with you? Are you ready for school to start?"

Lying back on the bed, she sighed. "Not really. I'm just ready to graduate so I can get out of here like you did."

Antoine laughed and then waved off his girlfriend, who was about to sit in his lap. Instead, she took a seat in a nearby chair. With a serious expression, he stood and walked over to the window.

"Patience, Denim. All you need to do is keep your head in your books."

"I know, but Mom and Dad are like prison wardens."

Antoine laughed. "Well, you'll appreciate them being hard on you when you get older."

"If you say so," she answered as she tried to keep from smiling.

"Nothing's changed with you since I left, has it?"

Denim knew exactly what her brother was talking about. She was still a virgin and planned to keep it that way, at least for now.

"No, Antoine! Nothing's changed. You know I would tell you if I was even considering something like that. Why did you ask?"

He picked up his Pepsi and took a sip before answering her. "Mom told me that you and Dré seemed to be a little tighter than you used to be. What's up with that?"

Rolling her eyes, she sat up and twirled a strand of her hair around her finger. "Your parents have me on serious lockdown, Antoine. It would be a miracle if they let Dré within ten feet of me. They let you do everything when you were my age, but I can't do anything or go anywhere."

Antoine sat down in a nearby chair and crossed his legs. Antoine was not only Denim's brother; he was her best friend too. At nearly six feet, three inches tall, he had been able to intimidate all the boys in their neighborhood that tried to get close to his sister—except Dré, which made Antoine admire him. He knew Dré was a good kid and would be good to his sister if, and only if, he got his life together and out of the environment he was living in.

Antoine and Denim looked very much alike. He had a way with the ladies, and he could see that she was drawing a lot of attention from the boys. Antoine had smooth brown skin, broad shoulders, and chiseled abs. He wore his hair in short twists and kept his goatee neatly trimmed. His eyes were dark brown and when he smiled, one dimple appeared on his cheek.

"Slow down, Denim. I warned you before I left for college that things might be like this. It's not always fair, but it's because you're a girl. I don't want to have to kill someone for putting their hands on you, and Mom and Daddy are just trying to protect you."

"That's cool, Antoine, but they're going to have to trust me at some point. It's not like I want to go clubbing all the time. I just want to go to a party every now and then and hang out with my friends."

"Well, you do understand that trust has to be earned, don't you?"

"Yeah, I guess." She pouted.

"Speaking of trust, what's this I hear about a shooting at a party down at the rec center last night?"

Denim put her hand over her eyes in disbelief. "Dang! How did you find out so quickly?"

"I know people," he said, laughing. "Remember?"

Denim laughed along with her brother, and then suddenly became silent. Antoine became even more serious with their conversation.

"Were you there?"

Denim remained quiet.

"Denim! Were you there?" he demanded to know.

She bit her nails and pleaded with her brother. "Please, Antoine, don't tell Mom and Dad. I was there, but only for a few minutes. Dré helped me sneak out of the house so I could go for one dance. It was his birthday, and some fool started shooting."

Angry, Antoine asked his girlfriend to leave the room before he went totally off on Denim.

"Denim! I'm seriously thinking about getting on a plane so I can come home and kick your butt! Have you lost your damn mind? Do you have any idea what Mom and Dad will do to you if they find out you were there? Don't you know you could've been killed? Damn, Denim! I can't believe you sometimes, and you're going to talk about trust?"

Denim knew she was in serious trouble with her brother. He always looked after her when they were growing up. Even from afar he was still trying to protect her.

"I'm sorry!" she whimpered through her tears.

"You're sorry? I'm going to kick Dré's butt too! You're acting like some love-starved fool. Why would take a chance like that? Are you sure you haven't let him touch you?"

"It's not Dré's fault, so leave him out of this. I wanted to go to the party, Antoine, and I told you I haven't done anything with Dré or any guy."

Antoine tried to calm himself. He couldn't believe Denim had pulled a stunt like this on him.

"Then what's going on with you, Denim? Is Dré putting some pressure on you?"

"No," she replied.

He took a deep breath. "Have you been thinking about it?" he asked.

"I think about it sometimes," she admitted.

"Well, that's all you better do is think about it. Your body is a temple, and guys will use you if you let them, so don't fall for that trick. They'll tell you what you want to hear and then some. Don't let them get in your head. You stay focused on your future, and when you're thirty years old, then maybe you can seriously think about it."

Denim laughed. "Thirty, huh?"

Antoine joined in her laughter. "You know what I mean. I'm serious, sis. Don't rush yourself through life. I love you, and I don't want you to get hurt."

"I know. I love you, too. Are you still mad at me?"

"Hell, yeah, but you know I can't stay mad at you forever. Look, you'd better stay low-key for a while. I'm sure you already know there is a fifty-fifty chance that Mom and Dad will find out you were there anyway, so be cool."

"I hope not, because if they do, I'm dead."

"Don't say I didn't warn you. I'm sure a lot of people were there, and not all of them knew you snuck out of the house to be at that party."

Denim thought about what her brother was saying. She knew he was right, and it made her very nervous. She knew in her heart that the best thing for her to do was to go ahead and tell her mom and dad the truth, and maybe she wouldn't be punished for the rest of her life.

"Antoine, can I ask you something?"

"Sure."

"Do you know anything about Dré messing around with drugs?"

"Yeah, I used to see him and his little punk friends in the park smoking. Why? Has he offered some to you?"

"No! I told him he would have to leave that stuff alone if he ever wanted me to kick it with him."

"Good for you!" Antoine said, laughing. "I hope he listens. He's a hell of a ball player, and doing it could end his career before it got started."

"Mom told me to stay away from him because she heard that he smokes."

"Do what she says, Denim. Seeing him at school should be enough for you. You don't want any more heat brought down on you."

Denim walked over to her computer and turned it on.

"You're right. So you think I should go ahead and tell them I was at that party?"

"That's on you, sis. I mean, that's something you're going to have to decide for yourself. I can't do that for you. But I will tell you this: Don't do anything like that ever again. Do you hear me?"

"I won't. I miss you, Antoine."

"I miss you too, Denim. I'll see you at Thanksgiving."

"I can't wait! Hey! Are you still fooling around with that girl from Chicago?"

He blushed. "Yeah, we're still together. Why do you ask?"

"Do you like her?"

He rubbed his hand across his chin and hesitated. "She's cool."

"How are your summer classes coming along?"

"They're good," he replied.

"Well, I guess I'd better let you go study. You are getting some studying done, aren't you, young man?"

He laughed out loud. "Yes, Denim, I'm studying very hard this summer. You sound like Mom now." They laughed together. "When Dad gets in, tell him I said hello and that I'll call him tomorrow."

"I will. I love you, Antoine."

"I love you too, Denim. See ya."

"Bye."

Denim hung up the telephone and sat on her bed, quietly contemplating whether she should tell her mom and dad she snuck out to Dré's party. She fell back on her bed and mumbled to herself, "I can't believe I'm considering turning myself in, but it would be worse if they found out on their own. I can't win!"

Antoine hung up the telephone and sat there in deep thought about his sister. Even though he talked to her almost every day, he still worried about her.

His girlfriend, Danielle, poked her head inside his room and smiled.

"Am I allowed back in the room yet?"

Smiling, he picked up one of his textbooks and opened it. "Yeah, sorry about that, Danielle. I needed to holler at my sister."

Sitting next to him, she put her arm around his shoulder and caressed his cheek. "That's an understatement. I could hear you yelling at her from the hallway. Is she okay?"

"She's going through some things at home, but she's cool," he revealed.

"Good! Now, can I please have a kiss before I leave you to your studying?"

Throwing his book aside, he pulled her into his lap and kissed her.

Danielle was a beautiful young woman, and she was very understanding, unlike his previous girlfriends. She was a native of Chicago, but had the charm of a Southern girl. She wore her hair short like Halle Berry, and had flawless skin. Her fair complexion hardly required any makeup. She did wear a little eyeliner and lipstick, but left the rest of her skin natural.

"Hmmm. That was very nice, Mr. Mitchell."

"I second that," he said before swatting her on the hip.

Standing, Danielle grabbed her book bag. "I'll call you later. Don't study too hard."

"Same to you, babe. Wait! Let me walk you back to your dorm."

He picked up his keys, and they headed out the door together.

Chapter Six

Samuel Mitchell pulled into his driveway and into the garage right on time. He was happy to finally get home because he'd missed his two favorite women. Exiting the car, he stretched and yawned. He popped the trunk, grabbed his luggage, and headed inside the house. When he opened the kitchen door, he was nearly knocked down by Denim.

"Welcome home, Daddy!"

Smiling, he set down his luggage and hugged her. "I'm glad to see you too, sweetheart."

Hugging him tightly, Denim buried her face in his chest. "Daddy, I hope that was your last out-of-town trip."

"So do I, rugrat. So do I."

Valessa stood back and let her daughter greet her father. She knew Denim missed him very much. Finally,

Samuel reached out for Valessa and pulled her into his arms, kissing her.

"Good afternoon, Mrs. Mitchell."

"Welcome home, Samuel. How was your trip?"

"Too long and too boring. Next time, you guys have to come with me."

She picked up one of his bags and headed toward the stairs. "It will be our pleasure."

"Dinner smells great!" Samuel said as he picked up his larger bag.

"I'll get it ready for you, Daddy," Denim said as she picked up a plate.

"Let me get a hot shower and I'll be right back down."

"Oh, Daddy! Antoine called earlier. He said to tell you hello and that he would call you tomorrow."

"Is everything okay with him?" Samuel asked before stepping out into the hallway.

"Antoine's just fine," Valessa said as she walked past her husband. "Come on so you can change into something more comfortable."

"Go ahead, babe. I'll be right up."

"Okay," Valessa replied before climbing the stairs.

Samuel stepped back into the kitchen. "Denim, I bought something for you, but I'll give it to you after dinner."

"Thanks, Daddy."

He kissed her forehead. "You're welcome, sweetheart. Thanks for fixing my plate. I'll be right back down." Samuel disappeared into the hallway and headed up the stairs.

Denim had always been a daddy's girl, and being almost sixteen wouldn't change a thing.

After dinner, Denim's parents relaxed in the family room while Denim entertained her best friend, Patrice, in her room. Patrice danced around the room to a video that was playing on TV.

"Girl, have you heard any more about the shooting at Dré's party?"

Bopping her head to the music, Denim replied, "No, and I wish everyone would stop talking about it. I'll be in big trouble if my parents find out I was there. I talked to Antoine about it, and he said it's up to me to decide if I should go ahead and tell them the truth. He said there's a slim possibility they won't kill me."

Patrice stopped dancing for a moment and stared at Denim. "Girl, I can't believe you're even considering it. Either way, you're going to be grounded for the rest of your life. Don't you want to go out for cheerleader?"

"You know I do."

"Well, if you tell them, they might not let you. Just think about it before you shoot yourself in the foot. Okay?"

Patrice always had a way with words. Denim couldn't help but laugh at her analysis of the situation.

"I will," she announced before she changed the channel to another station.

Out of breath, Patrice fell back on Denim's bed. She grabbed one of Denim's stuffed animals. "Is Antoine ready to marry me yet?"

Denim rolled her eyes and laughed. "Girl, give it up. Antoine is not going to mess with your jail-bait butt."

They laughed together, then discussed which CD they wanted to listen to. Once they decided on one, Denim slid it into her stereo and turned up the volume. Patrice immediately started dancing again. "Girl, that's my jam! Oh, and Antoine might not mess with me, but the question is . . . are you going to get busy with Dré?"

Denim threw a teddy bear at Patrice. "Dré and I are going to take things slow."

"Sure you are. I see the way he looks at you, and Dré ain't thinking about taking anything slow with you," Patrice announced as she snapped her fingers at Denim.

"Whatever!"

"Play dumb if you want to, Denim," Patrice said as she motioned for Denim to dance with her, "but Dré is hot for you."

Denim started dancing to the beat with Patrice.

"Dré knows my mom heard the rumors about him messing with drugs. She's not about to let me do anything with him. They have me on serious lockdown, Patrice. I probably won't get to go out with anybody until I'm twenty-one, and even then, it won't be Dré. They think his parents are doing something illegal. I overheard them talking about it one night."

"Girl, my parents said the same thing!" Patrice said, waving off Denim's comments. "Do you think what people are saying is true?"

Denim stopped dancing and turned down the music.

"I don't know what to think anymore."

Patrice also stopped dancing. "Don't you want to go out with Dré?"

Denim blushed. "You know I do. Patrice, don't tell anybody, but the other day he asked me if I loved him."

"Are you serious?" Patrice yelled as she gave Denim a high five. "What did you say?"

Denim bit her bottom lip and hesitated before answering. "I told him I did. I also told him that he needed to leave that drug mess alone because he's an athlete and it's not good for him. If he got arrested, his life would be over."

Patrice fell back on the bed and squealed.

"Denim, you have Dré in the palm of your hand, and you don't even realize it. That fool is in love! Most guys would've told you to kiss their ass, but not Dré. He wants you, Denim."

Patrice continued to laugh while Denim threw pillows at her to try to calm her down.

"Stop it! I don't feel like I have anybody in the palm of my hand."

"Whatever! Believe what you want to. Denim, do you realize that you have the cutest and most popular guy in school yearning for you?" Patrice pointed out.

Denim blushed. "He has to stop with the drugs, Patrice, or all of this means nothing to me."

"So, do you think he's going to stop?" Patrice asked as she stacked Denim's pillows back on the bed.

"I don't know. He said he would. If he cares about me like he says, he will."

"Well, you'd better watch your back because there

are a lot of girls at school who will take Dré like he is right now."

"You don't have to tell me," Denim said solemnly. "I just hope he changes and soon."

"I second that!" Patrice said as she gave Denim another high five.

Downstairs, Valessa and Samuel relaxed in the family room.

"Did I miss anything exciting while I was away?" Samuel asked as he caressed his wife's hand.

Valessa laid her head on his shoulder and answered. "Sort of. Your daughter had a fit because I wouldn't let her go to Dré's birthday party down at the recreation center."

He frowned. "Did she disrespect you? Because if she did, I'll talk to her and get her straight."

"She got a little attitude with me, but you know me. I can handle Miss Thang."

"You did right, sweetheart. I'm still hearing people talk about Dré messing around with drugs. He seems to be a good kid, but he just doesn't seem to have any proper guidance from his parents. That's what's wrong with a lot of kids Denim's age. They don't have any decent parents to teach them right from wrong."

"We're so fortunate, Samuel," Valessa whispered. "I know there are a lot of kids out there who are on the fence and could go either way. I'm not saying our kids don't have their issues, but things could be so much worse."

Samuel nodded in agreement. "That's why we have to

continue to talk to the kids and keep that line of communication open with them."

Valessa made eye contact with him. "I agree," she said.

"So, Denim thought she would push you a little this weekend?"

"What she did was come close to getting clocked upside the head by me."

They laughed together for a moment. Picking up her glass of iced tea, Valessa took a sip.

"Did you know a kid got shot at Dré's party? From what I've heard, he'll live, but they said he might be paralyzed from the waist down."

"That's crazy. I'm so glad Denim wasn't there."

"So am I, and that's the main reason I wouldn't let her go. Oh! By the way, I wish you could've seen the way Denim and Dré were looking at and touching each other the other day."

Samuel frowned and set down his iced tea. "What do you mean, touching?"

"Calm down, honey. Denim was cleaning out the garage and Dré came down to talk to her. At first they were just talking, and then I saw them holding hands. He kissed her on the forehead a couple of times, but that was about it. Their body language was what made me so nervous."

"I'll talk to him."

"Wait a minute, Samuel. I don't think that's a good idea."

"Denim is our daughter, and if they're touching and

kissing, I need to talk to Dré and let him know where we stand."

Valessa sighed. "Well, Denim's had the talk, so I just pray she uses her head. You know she's almost sixteen, going on twenty-one."

"Don't remind me. And until I know different and have a chance to talk to Dré, I don't want her around him. Agreed?"

"Agreed," she replied as they touched their glasses together.

He winked at her and then laughed.

"What's so funny?" she asked.

"Valessa, do me a favor and think back to when you were sixteen. Your hormones were bouncing off the walls just like mine. Our son was no different when he was Denim's age either. Actually, I think he was worse."

"You got that right. That boy was trying to date every girl in a ten-mile radius."

"But this is my baby girl, Valessa."

"I know, Samuel, and if it were up to me, I'd lock her in her room until she was forty, but you know we can't do that. Just talk to Dré and we'll go from there. And I'll talk to Denim again to reinforce our understanding about boys."

Valessa stood and picked up Samuel's empty glass.

"I hope we're doing the right thing. I'll refill your glass."

He looked at his watch. "Thanks, babe. By the way, it's getting late. I'm going up to get Denim so we can drive Patrice home."

"Okay. Be careful and hurry back."

* * *

On the drive back from Patrice's house, Samuel looked over at Denim, who was staring out the window in deep thought.

Without taking his eyes off the road, Samuel asked, "So, what have you been up to over the past few days?"

"Not much, Daddy," Denim answered, looking down at her hands.

"Are you sure? I heard you were upset about not being able to go to Dré's party."

Denim glanced over at her father. "I was upset, Daddy. Mom wouldn't let me go, but I tried to tell her that only kids my age would be there."

"Sweetheart, it's okay to have disagreements with your mother, but I don't ever want you to disrespect her. Do you understand?"

"Yes, sir," she whispered.

"Your mother and I have our reasons for not letting you do some of the things you want to do. It's not that we're trying to take away your fun; we're trying to protect you."

Denim looked over at her father and nodded. "I know, Daddy. It's just that sometimes it doesn't seem fair. I'll be sixteen in a couple of months."

"Life is not always fair, and in some cases, there's nothing you can do about it."

Denim heard what her father was saying, but it still didn't seem fair to her. As she sat there in deep thought, he jarred her out of her trance.

"What's going on between you and Dré?"

Denim immediately started grinning. "Nothing, Daddy. Why do you ask?"

"According to your mother, she thought it looked like you two were more than just friends the other day."

Her father's comment alerted Denim to the fact that her mother had seen her talking to Dré in the driveway. "We were just talking, Daddy."

Samuel changed lanes and said, "That's not what I heard. Has he kissed you?"

"Daddy!"

"Don't *Daddy* me. Has he kissed you?"

"Yeah, but it was no big deal."

"On the lips?" he asked.

"Just a little peck here and there, Daddy, but it's mostly been on the cheek and forehead."

Chills ran over Samuel's body.

"Nothing, huh?"

"It was no big deal, Daddy," she said without making eye contact with him.

Samuel swallowed hard before asking his next question. "Have you guys done anything else besides kiss?"

Denim lowered her head with embarrassment. "I can't believe you're asking me this, Daddy."

"I want to know, Denim. Besides, I'm your father, and you should be able to tell me anything, even if it will make me age ten years. That goes for your mother, too," he said in a semi-joking manner.

"No, Daddy!" she answered, smiling. "I haven't done

anything with Dré but kiss him, so you and Mom can relax. Okay?"

Samuel laughed. "Good! Now tell me about the drugs. Is Dré really messing around with that stuff?"

Pulling the mirror down so she could apply lip-gloss, she answered, "I don't know, Daddy."

Samuel pulled up to a stop sign and stopped. "What about you? Have you tried any drugs?"

She closed the mirror and frowned. "No way! I can't stand the way that stuff smells. It stinks!"

He drove through the intersection and turned onto their street. "You do know that all drugs don't have to be smoked, don't you?"

"I know a few kids at school who take some kind of pills. I don't hang with anyone like that."

Nodding with satisfaction, Samuel pulled into their garage.

"Denim, if you ever feel pressured by Dré or any of your friends to do something you know we disapprove of, please come and talk to us. Okay?"

"Yes, Daddy."

"Be careful at school, too, because sometimes kids will put something in your drink or food just to get you hooked."

"I'll be careful, Daddy. I promise."

"Good. Come on and help your old man put the trash on the curb."

She unbuckled her seatbelt, climbed out of the car, and grabbed a garbage can.

* * *

Down the street, Dré's father walked into his room. "Dré, I need you to make some pickups for me."

Dré pulled the iPod earphones out of his ears and sat up on the side of his bed. "What did you say, Daddy?"

"I said I need you to make some pickups for me. Reno can't do it, and I have somewhere I have to be. The addresses and contact names are inside this bag."

Dré frowned. "Daddy, I don't think it's a good idea for me to get involved with your business."

Angry, his father asked, "Do you live here?"

"Yes, sir," he replied.

"Then you're involved. Now get moving. Time is money," he said as he turned to walk away.

Dré stood up and pleaded with his Dad. "Daddy, if I get caught, I could get arrested and expelled from school and blow any chance I have of going to college. Is that what you want?"

He father turned to him and said, "What I want is for you to do what I told you to do. Don't worry. Everything will be all right. Everybody knows you're my kid, so ain't nobody gon' mess with you."

Dré could see that his father meant business and there was no reasoning with him, so he grabbed the bag and angrily walked past his father and out the door. Once outside, he pulled the piece of paper out of the bag and studied the addresses before he jumped into his car and drove off down the block.

Address after address, Dré collected money as his father had instructed. Some of the locations he entered were dark, smoky, and seedy, making him a little fearful, but he wasn't about to show it. Business after business, Dré entered and exited, and every time he did, he noticed a police car parked nearby. It made him very uneasy, but he kept going. On his last stop, two officers outside a pool hall approached Dré.

"Hey, son, are you Patterson's kid?"

Dré kept his cool. The last thing he wanted was a run-in with the local police. He replied, "Yes, sir."

The other officer spoke next. "You play basketball at Freedman, don't you?"

Again, Dré replied, "Yes, sir."

They stared at Dré and then the book bag he had over his shoulder. Not wanting to make any sudden movement, Dré said, "Well, if you would excuse me, I need to be getting home."

The officers stepped back, allowing Dré to open his car door.

"Drive safely, kid."

Dré closed the door and buckled his seat belt. "I will."

The officers watched as Dré pulled away from the curb. As he drove down the street, he looked back in his rearview mirror to see if the police were following him. Luckily, they weren't, but he had a feeling they knew exactly what he was doing. He also felt like the only reason they didn't bust him was because he played ball.

* * *

It took nearly two hours for Dré to collect all the money. Once he returned home, he angrily dropped the bag at his father's feet. "Here's your money, Dad. I hope this is the first and last time you ask me to do something crazy like this. You could've gotten me arrested. Two cops stopped me outside the pool hall."

Dré's father set his cigarette down in the ashtray. "What cops?"

"I don't know, two cops!" he yelled.

"What did they look like?" his Dad asked.

Dré went on to describe the police officers.

"Son, I know you don't understand why I do what I do. In time, you'll understand just how far I'll go to take care of my family."

"Why can't you get a regular job like other dads?" Dré asked.

"Because I already have a job," he replied as he took a puff of his cigarette. "One day, I'll be able to explain everything to you. Now, this discussion is over, and don't worry; I won't need you to make any more pickups for me, but I appreciate you helping me out tonight."

Dré stared at his father in disbelief. All he wanted was a father he wasn't ashamed of, but according to his father, that was asking too much of him. Disgusted, Dré sighed. "Can I go now?"

"Yes, you can step, but before you go, I want you to know that I do love you, even though you might not think I do."

Dré walked out of the room without responding. Before turning the corner, he watched his father pick up the book bag and pull out stacks of money and small pieces of paper. Dré's father was what is known as a "numbers man." He ran an illegal, underground lottery and gambling business and had made thousands from it. The sad thing was that his father had a brilliant business mind; he just wasn't using it honestly. Instead, he settled for continuing his reckless lifestyle, which could eventually cost them everything.

Upset by his conversation with his dad, Dré walked out of the house and climbed inside his car. He drove to a nearby park and called DeMario. It was late, but the lights on the basketball court were still on. Within minutes, DeMario pulled up beside him and the two got out of their vehicles.

"What's got you out so late tonight, Dré? You don't look so good."

Dré popped open the trunk of his car and grabbed his basketball. He threw it to DeMario and sighed. "It's my dad. He's trippin' again."

DeMario dribbled the basketball over to the court and shot a three-point shot, hitting nothing but net. He turned to Dré and threw the ball back to him so he could take a shot. "What did he do?"

Dré dribbled the ball through his legs before releasing a shot. "I had to make his pickups for him."

"Where was his boy, Reno?" DeMario asked. "Don't he normally do it?"

"Don't know. He said something about Reno being

tied up or something. I hated doing it too. You should've seen the way those old dudes were looking at me when I walked in to collect. My dad must've told them I was making the pickup because none of them hesitated. It didn't help that two cops approached me outside the pool hall."

DeMario played a little defense on Dré and then stole the ball. He drove to the basket and dunked the ball. "That's messed up. Weren't you scared of getting busted or robbed?"

"Hell yeah! I told my dad don't ever ask me to do it again."

DeMario looked over at Dré and asked, "I'm sure he didn't like you talking back to him, did he?"

Dré shook his head and said, "Nah, he didn't. I can't wait to turn eighteen so I can get out of Freedman."

DeMario shot the ball and said, "You and me both. Forget about your dad for a while and let's play ball."

"Music to my ears." Dré cranked up the music on the car radio and the two began to play the first of several games before heading home.

Chapter Seven

A few weeks later, Denim and her friends were happy to be going back school. Denim made cheerleader for the upcoming basketball season and she couldn't wait to cheer for Dré. Going back to school was bittersweet because she had gotten used to sleeping in; however, she was anxious to see all her friends again. Another good thing was that the beginning of school also meant new clothes and accessories. Unfortunately, since the dress code was so strict, some of the more fashionable attire was not allowed in school. She was also hopeful that the Mustang her father was working on for her would finally be restored to its original luster and condition and she'd be able to roll in style.

On the first day of school, the halls were buzzing with activity. Excitement was in the air, and Denim and her friends were anxious to start this year off with a bang.

Denim wore a pair of Apple Bottoms jeans and a short-sleeve shirt with the Apple Bottoms logo on it. While she worked the combination to her locker, her classmates mingled in the hallway, and the sound of lockers opening and closing radiated throughout the area. Denim watched as classmates laughed and hugged upon seeing each other for the first time since May.

One of the first friendly faces she saw was Patrice. She came running up to her, loud as usual.

"Denim, I can't believe they really changed the dress code this year. They won't let us wear short tops anymore! That's all I have!"

"I tried to warn you," Denim said as she pulled open her locker door. "You knew they were going to stop all of that video vixen attire anyway. Personally, I'm glad. At least we're not in uniforms like the schools in other states."

"I guess you're right," Patrice replied while popping her gum loudly. "So, have you seen your man yet?"

Denim put some of her textbooks inside her locker and mounted a mirror on the inside door before closing it. "My man?" Denim asked. "Are you talking about Dré?"

"You're so crazy, Denim! Yes, your man! Why are you acting like you two don't have anything going on?"

"It's because we don't, actually," Denim answered as she leaned against her locker door. "I haven't seen or heard from Dré since the night of his party."

About that time, Denim's math teacher walked over to them.

"Good morning, Ms. Maston."

"It's nice to see you girls." Ms. Maston tugged at Patrice's top and said, "Patrice, I take it that you got a copy of the new school dress code?"

"Yes, ma'am."

"Then we won't see any more of these blouses at school anymore, correct?"

Patrice folded her arms across her chest and nodded. Ms. Maston turned to Denim. "Denim, I'm looking forward to having you in my class this year. I might need your help tutoring some of the other kids if that sounds like something you might want to do. It'll be worth some extra credit points for you."

Denim's eyes lit up. "Yes, ma'am, I might like that."

Ms. Maston sighed and looked Patrice up and down before walking off. "Have a good year, ladies."

"You too, Ms. Maston," Denim replied.

Patrice watched Ms. Maston walk farther down the hall. She turned up her nose and said, "Ms. Maston makes me sick. She's always putting people on blast, especially me."

Denim giggled and said, "It's your fault, Patrice. I told you not to wear that top. Besides, if you didn't give her a reason to put you on blast, she wouldn't do it."

Patrice waved her off. "Whatever. Forget about Ms. Maston. I want to get back to you and Dré."

Denim rolled her eyes because she knew that Patrice wasn't going to drop the subject anytime soon.

"Correct me if I'm wrong, but didn't you tell me that you told Dré you loved him?"

Denim pulled her lip gloss out of her purse and reapplied it. "Yes, but that's as far as it went except for the night of the party when we danced."

"That's cool, Denim, but you and I both know that Dré has been laying low because of what went down at his party."

"And how do you know? Did DeMario tell you or something?"

Patrice popped a stick of gum into her mouth. "No, DeMario won't tell me anything, but I did ask."

"He could've texted me or something. Dré has no excuse for not contacting me."

About that time, Dré, DeMario, and another young man turned the corner, walking in Denim and Patrice's direction. Patrice grabbed Denim by the arm.

"Oh, Denim! There he is! Damn, they look hot!"

Denim turned around and noticed Dré and his friends getting a lot of attention from all the females who were in the hallway. Dré looked as handsome as ever in his G-Unit jeans, T-shirt, and light blue button-down shirt. He spotted Denim in the crowd and immediately made his way toward her.

"Here he comes," Patrice leaned over and whispered. "I'll see you later, girl. Handle your business."

Reaching for Patrice's arm, Denim tried her best to keep her from leaving her alone with Dré.

"Come back here, Patrice!" she yelled, but to no avail.

Laughing, Patrice went farther down the hall, but within sight of the pair. Dré finally made his way over to Denim. He pulled her into his arms and gave her a big hug.

"Denim, seeing you every day makes coming to school worthwhile. You are looking fine as ever, girl."

She dismissed his compliment, backed out of his embrace, and immediately lit into him.

"Listen, Dré', I know you can't come to my house because of my parents, but why haven't you called or emailed me? Are you upset with me about something? Did I do something wrong?"

"No, Denim, I'm not upset with you, I—"

She cut him off and continued her rant. "Oh, I guess you doing your little disappearing act is just a preview of what you'll do to me if I ever let you get closer to me, huh? I don't deserve to be treated like that, Dré. I thought you cared about me and I thought you wanted to hook up with me, but I guess I was wrong."

Dré lowered his head and took in Denim's harsh words, because he deserved every one of them. He had pulled away from her physically, but it wasn't for the reasons she suspected. He was trying to protect her. Not one day passed since the shooting at his party that he didn't think about her or want to call her.

"Are you done?" he asked.

"Maybe," she answered sarcastically with her arms folded across her chest. Dré leaned against the lockers and let out a loud breath before explaining his absence to her.

"Denim, I didn't want to stay away from you, but I had to. It was the hardest thing I ever had to do. I had a lot of soul searching to do after that stuff went down at my party, and I have some stuff going on at home. I didn't want any distractions."

"Oh, is that what I am now? A distraction?"

Denim started to walk away, but Dré grabbed her arm, stopping her.

"Listen to me! You're not a distraction. The police have been over at our house asking a lot of questions about the shooting. I didn't want to bring any heat to you and your family, so I pulled up."

"You could've told me or sent word by DeMario."

"You're right, but I haven't been thinking straight lately. These past few weeks have been hell for me. I've stopped smoking and I've been working out at the gym almost nonstop. I thought about everything you said to me and everything that could've happened to you that night. Between you and me, I guess you can say I've been scared straight.

"Denim, you're the best thing that ever happened to me. If you don't hear from me, it's not because I'm avoiding you. I love you."

Denim looked up at him. She needed to look into his eyes to see if he was being sincere.

"What are you saying, Dré?" she whispered.

A couple of guys walked over and greeted Dré with a handshake and hug. After they passed by, Dré continued.

"I'm saying you're more important to me than getting high, and I'll do whatever it takes to stay clean, graduate, and get out of this town."

Denim watched Dré's facial expression. He'd never

looked so sincere. She was beginning to feel bad about yelling at him.

Denim reached up and gently tugged on his ear. Dré leaned down closer to her, but she still had to get up on her tiptoes in order to whisper into his ear. "I'm sorry I yelled at you. You must think I'm a nag. I bet you can't wait to get away from me, huh?"

He smiled and touched her chin lovingly. "You're not a nag, Denim, and when I leave Freedman, I hope you'll want to go with me."

Denim didn't know what to say. It was obvious that Dré had done some type of soul-searching; she just prayed he meant it and would be able to stick to it.

"I don't know, Dré. Actions speak louder than words. I want to believe you mean what you're saying, but I don't know. My parents are not keen on the thought of us hanging out together."

"I'm not throwing any bull at you, Denim. I just hope you haven't given up on me."

She took his hand into hers. "You know I would never give up on you. Besides, if I thought you were a lost cause, I would've walked away from you a long time ago. I just hope you're serious about everything."

He looked down at her and smiled. "I couldn't be more serious. Like you said, I have to think about my basketball career and my life."

Denim blushed and playfully bumped against him with her hips. "I've missed talking to you these past few weeks."

Dré reached over and played with a curl dangling

next to her ear. "So have I. . . . Denim, I've also missed something else."

Anika, a girl who was notorious for her devious ways, walked over and rudely interrupted the couple. She turned up her nose at Denim and then smiled at Dré. As she straightened his collar, she snuggled up to him. "Dré, this shade of blue looks so hot on you."

He reached up and removed her hands, knowing that Anika's actions weren't sitting well with Denim. "Thank you, Anika. With the new dress code, I guess you'll have a hard time showing off your body this year, huh?"

Denim gave Anika an angry look. "Yeah, Anika, since showing off your body seems to be the only thing you have going for you."

Denim's jealousy only fueled Anika's motives. Anika wrapped her arms around Dré's waist. "Forget you, Denim. As long as Dré's looking, I'm going to show off my body any way I please."

Dré raised his hands in the air and said, "Back up, Anika. You're being foul."

Anika winked at Denim and then looked up at Dré. "You know you like the way my body feels against yours."

Dré was angry now, and just as he reached down to try to get out of her grasp, Denim grabbed her arm and pulled her away from Dré. She pushed her against a row of lockers, causing a scene. People in the hall took notice and started jeering.

Denim put her finger in Anika's face and said, "Don't

you ever disrespect me again! You saw Dré talking to me, and you also know that he don't want any part of you. Don't mess with me, Anika!"

"I'm not scared of you, and you need to get your finger out of my face!" Anika yelled.

"You better be scared of me, and I'll move my finger when I'm good and ready to move my finger!" Denim yelled.

At that moment, Dré saw one of the Resource Officers coming down the hallway. Dré grabbed Denim by the wrist. "Chill, babe. A Resource Officer is coming."

Dré pulled Denim back across the hall, but she was still able to give Anika a look that could freeze hell.

"What's going on here?" the Resource Officer asked. "Break it up!"

The crowd dispersed without revealing information.

"Get to class!" he yelled before continuing on down the hallway.

Anika joined her entourage and disappeared through the crowd.

Dré sighed and said, "That was crazy. I thought you were going to wild out on Anika."

"She's a slut and a bully. I hope you didn't like what she did."

Dré frowned. "Hell no! She only did that to mess with you, but I guess she found out you were not the one."

"I hate girls like her," Denim admitted. "I don't know what came over me. I could've gotten expelled on the first day of school."

"I wouldn't let that happen. If I had to, I would've taken the heat from the Resource Officer."

"You would do that for me?" she asked.

He touched her chin so she would look at him. "I'd do that and a lot more."

Denim smiled and then looked away without responding.

"Denim, what would you do if I kissed you right now?"

She looked at him in amazement, unable to respond. Before she could answer him, he lowered his head and kissed her firmly on the lips, and lingered there. Overwhelmed and breathless, Denim took a step back and looked around the hallway to see if anyone had seen them. Unfortunately, everyone had, and they clapped and cheered in response.

"Why did you do that?" Denim asked, embarrassed by all the attention.

"Because I love you, Denim," he said, smiling. "It's as simple as that, and by the way, I can't wait to see you in that short cheerleader skirt cheering for me."

Denim's face was hot and flushed now. "Dré, stop. You're embarrassing me."

He burst out laughing and hugged her again. "I'm just letting these guys around here know that you're my girl and they bet' not step to you."

"Are you for real?" Denim asked. "You did that for show?"

"You did the same thing with Anika. Otherwise, you wouldn't have responded like you did."

What Dré said was the truth. She wanted all the girls at Freedman to know Dré was spoken for and all hers.

"Whatever, Dré," she said, blushing.

Dré looked at his watch and said, "I'll be over to your house this evening. I think I need to clear up some things with your parents."

Startled, Denim stepped out of his embrace. "My parents? What are you going to talk to them about?"

He started backing down the hallway to rejoin his friends. "Us. Plus, I have something I want to give you."

She motioned for him to come back closer to her. "Are you sure you want to do that?"

"I'm sure. I'm not wasting any more time, Denim. I'm really into you, and I want to do this the right way."

"What do you have for me?" she asked as she clutched her books to her chest.

"You'll have to wait and see," he said as he turned and walked down the hallway.

"Dré!" she called out to him.

"Patience, babe. I'll be over after school," he said, laughing.

Dré joined up with his friends and disappeared around the corner. Denim was frozen in her spot until Patrice ran up to her.

"Girl, everybody saw you jack Anika and Dré kissing you. You have some pissed off sistas in this school, especially Anika."

Denim slowly walked down the hallway with Patrice.

"Forget Anika and those other girls. I don't care what they think. Anika started it anyway. All I did was finish it. As far as the kiss, Dré was the one who made all the moves."

Patrice put her arm around Denim's shoulder. "You're right, and Anika got everything she deserves. Her plan backfired on her. She was trying to embarrass you and ending up getting embarrassed."

Denim and Patrice walked into their history class and sat down.

"Anika and her friends can hate on me all they want to. If they have a problem with me and Dré hooking up, too bad!"

Patrice gave Denim a high five and smiled. She'd never seen her act so tough.

"Listen at you! I'm proud of you, Denim, but watch your back. You might have won the battle, but the war is just beginning. Those girls will do anything they can to come between you and Dré, especially after you went off on Anika in front of everybody."

Denim opened her notebook and frowned. "They can bring it on if they want to."

The history teacher walked into the classroom, so Patrice and Denim had to end their conversation. Denim sat there wondering if today was going to be the beginning of a dream, or a nightmare.

After school, Dré walked into the house and found his mother cooking dinner. He walked over to the stove to see what she was preparing. He reached up and grabbed a piece of meat. "That smells like pork chops."

She playfully spanked his hand and said, "It is. Now go wash your hands so you can eat."

Dré kissed her on the cheek and asked, "Where's your husband?"

She turned to him and put her hands on her hips. "You mean your father?"

"Whatever," he replied. "Until he starts acting like one, he's not going to be treated like one."

"Dré! Please try to get along with your father. He means well in spite of what he does."

Dré set his book bag in the chair and said, "Mom, I know you don't like it either. It's like Daddy doesn't care how his business will affect us if he gets caught."

She turned back to her oven and said, "That's where you're wrong, sweetheart. You'd be surprised how much your father protects and provides for us. I can't give you any details, but just know that you and I are protected if anything ever happens to him."

Dré stood there thinking about what his mother just revealed. He had no idea what she meant, and in reality, he didn't really want to know. All he wanted to do was have a life like other kids and have a father who was there for him in ways other than financially. He wanted to see his father in the stands cheering him on when he played basketball. He wanted his love and support more than money.

"Mom, can you save me a plate? After I finish my homework I'm going over to Denim's house for a little while."

She turned to him with a raised brow. "What's going on at the Mitchells'?"

Dré fumbled with his shirt. "Nothing much. I'm going to ask Mr. Mitchell if I can go out with Denim."

His mother smiled. "I knew it was coming. You and Denim have been close for years, and you've never shown a serious interest in any other girl. Denim's sweet and she has good manners, unlike a lot of those other fast girls you go to school with. Her parents are cool, too, so don't do anything to piss them off."

"I won't," he assured her.

"Do I need to have *the talk* with you again?"

Embarrassed, he blushed. "No, I'm cool. Denim means a lot to me, Mom. I wouldn't do anything to hurt her or mess up our lives."

She shook her spoon at him and said, "Then we're straight when I say no babies, right?"

He walked over and kissed his mother on the forehead. "No babies until I'm at least twenty-five."

"All right, now go on and get your homework done. I want to hear all about your visit when you get back."

Dré picked up his book bag and walked toward his room. "A'ight, Mom."

Later that evening, Dré walked up on Denim's porch and rang the doorbell.

Samuel answered the door and greeted him. "Hello, Dré. Come on in. Denim told us you might be coming over."

Dré shook Samuel's hand and said, "Thank you, sir."

"No problem at all. It'll give us a chance to talk. What's that you have under your arm?"

Raising the canvas, Dré showed Samuel the beautiful portrait he had painted of Denim. Samuel was very impressed with Dré's talent and eye for detail. Samuel took the painting out of Dré's hands so he could inspect it more closely.

"This is very nice, Dré. You really need to pursue this talent of yours. You're already an exceptional athlete. This could be something that could really put you on the map."

"I do love to paint, and I'll keep that in mind, sir."

Samuel walked toward the family room and motioned for Dré to follow.

"Good for you," Samuel said.

Dré followed Samuel into the family room. For the occasion, he was dressed in a pair of khaki cargo pants and a bright yellow Sean John shirt with a matching baseball hat that he took off when he entered the house. Denim and Valessa entered the room, causing Dré to smile when his eyes met with Denim's. He stood and walked over to greet Valessa respectfully.

"Hello, Mrs. Mitchell."

"Hello, Dré," Valessa said while shaking his hand. Then Dré turned to Denim and greeted her.

"Hey, Denim."

She blushed as she sat down on the loveseat next to him. "Hey, Dré."

Samuel held up the portrait so Valessa and Denim could see it.

"Look at the beautiful portrait Dré painted of Denim," Samuel said.

In awe, Denim and Valessa looked at the portrait. Denim was speechless as she stared at her likeness.

"This is absolutely gorgeous, Dré. How long did it take you to do this?" Valessa asked.

"I worked on it off and on for about two weeks."

"Well, it's beautiful. You captured every detail of our daughter's face," Valessa admitted with praise.

Denim looked over at Dré, and with a broad smile, she thanked him. "I knew you were good, but this is unbelievable. Thank you, Dré."

"You're welcome, Denim."

The connection between the two was electrifying, and the Mitchells saw it right before their eyes.

"Denim, why don't you go into the kitchen and check on dinner while your father and I have a little talk with Dré?"

Denim stood with the portrait in hand. Dré also stood, as a gesture of respect. Denim winked at Dré as she exited the room. She wanted to assure him that everything would be all right, but he wasn't worried.

Dré sat down opposite the Mitchells and waited for them to give him "the talk."

Samuel cleared his throat before speaking. "Dré, I'm actually glad you came over tonight because Valessa and I would like to know just where your relationship stands with Denim. We know you two have been friends for a long time, but lately it seems that the friendship has turned into something much more, and we have our concerns.

"Our concerns mostly consist of the rumors that you do drugs. We will not allow Denim around any of that kind of behavior."

Cool as a cucumber, Dré looked directly at Samuel and Valessa, and replied, "Mr. and Mrs. Mitchell, I'm not going to sit here and lie to you. The rumors you heard were true, but I want you to know that I've given all that up thanks to Denim. She made me see that it wasn't good for my health, and that it could ruin my life and my athletic career."

"How can we be sure you're telling us the truth?" Valessa asked with a frown.

Rubbing his head, Dré sighed. "I don't know, Mrs. Mitchell. You'll just have to trust me on it, because I would like the chance to go out with Denim."

"Trust is not to be taken lightly, Dré, and I hope you mean every word you're saying to us," Valessa explained. "Honesty and trust are two things we stress with our children, and when it's broken, there are unpleasant consequences."

"I understand that, Mrs. Mitchell. I've given up the drugs for several reasons, which includes the fact that I don't want to hurt my chances of getting into a good college and the NBA. The other reason is that I know it's not good for me. I care about Denim very much, and I know you expect her to date someone with the high standards you set for her. I want to be that guy, and I will do whatever it takes to get you to believe that I've changed."

"We hear you, Dré, but Denim is not allowed to date right now," Valessa said.

"I understand that, Mrs. Mitchell, but when the time comes, I hope you guys will give me a chance."

Samuel smiled and looked over at Valessa. While he planned to be the one doing all the talking, Valessa stepped up and did the honors. He knew Dré was surprising her with his manners and demeanor. He also remembered his past, when he was a teenager experimenting with marijuana and alcohol. He just didn't want to see another young man go down a path that could affect his life forever. Samuel was happy that Dré seemed to recognize the importance of protecting his health and future.

"Dré, I'm going to be straight with you, since it seems like you're being straight with us. I hate knowing you were ever involved with drugs. I'm going to take you at your word that all of that is behind you now. Denim is our only daughter, and we want nothing but the best for her, which means we don't want to become grandparents until she's grown and married. Do you understand where I'm coming from?"

"Yes, sir," he answered.

"Denim has always been taught to take care of herself," Samuel continued, "and we want you to understand that if we allow our daughter to date you, or any boy, if anything happens to her, you'll have us to deal with, and it won't be a pleasant experience. I can guarantee you that. Oh, and there's one more thing, and it regards your father. I know what he does, and once again, I don't want Denim anywhere near your house. Bullets don't have eyes, and God forbid someone decides to take revenge on your father in any way. I don't want Denim caught up in the middle of it. Understand?"

Dré looked at the Mitchells and politely said, "I understand, and I agree with you."

"Good," Samuel replied. "I'm glad we see eye to eye on the subject."

Dré waited to see if either of them had anything else to add before he responded. When it was quiet between them for a few seconds, he spoke.

"Believe me, Mr. and Mrs. Mitchell, I can't blame you for being worried about Denim hanging out with me, and you don't have to worry about me doing anything with Denim that could ruin her future. When it comes to the subject of my dad, I hate what he does too. I've tried to talk to him, but he won't listen."

Valessa smiled and said, "It sounds like you're the adult."

Dré scooted out on the edge of the loveseat. "I want you to know that I'll protect Denim with my life because she means that and more to me."

Hearing what sounded like Dré's confession of love for Denim sent chills down Valessa's spine. Dré clearly had strong feelings for their daughter. It was sweet and scary at the same time.

"Dré, remember you're only sixteen, and you and Denim have plenty of time to date before committing yourselves to each other. Just enjoy your time in high school, focus on college, and wait and see what life has in store for you. Okay?"

"I will. Thank you, Mrs. Mitchell."

Samuel stood. "I'm sure once Valessa and I have a chance to talk about this further and with your parents, we'll be able to make a clear decision on you guys dating when the time comes. So, with that settled, let's eat. I'm sure you're hungry by now."

Valessa also stood. Dré shook Samuel's hand, then Valessa's.

"Thank you for giving me a chance to talk to you guys, but I'm sorry I can't stay for dinner. My mother has my dinner waiting for me."

Samuel patted Dré on the shoulder. "I know it's short notice, Dré, but why don't you call your mother and see if it's okay if you have dinner with us? It'll give us more time to talk."

"Are you sure, Mr. Mitchell?"

"I'm sure."

Dré pulled out his cell phone as Valessa and Samuel walked ahead into the dining room to give him some privacy.

Dré called his mother as instructed. Even though she was a little disappointed, she appreciated him having the courtesy to call her. With her blessings, she allowed him to have dinner with the Mitchells. Dré entered the dining room and found Denim putting the last of the dishes out on the table. Laid out was a pork roast and potatoes, green beans, corn on the cob, and cornbread. Samuel was filling everyone's glasses while Valessa made sure there were plenty of napkins on the table.

"Wow! Everything looks delicious," Dré acknowledged when he saw all the food on the table.

Denim blushed and said, "Thank you, Dré."

Dré turned to the Mitchells and said, "My mom said it was okay for me to stay for dinner."

"That's nice, Dré, and for just for your information, Denim did most of the cooking," Valessa proudly revealed as she sat down.

Dré looked over at Denim and told her how impressed he was. Once everyone was seated, they joined hands and Samuel blessed the food.

After dinner, Dré and Denim sat out on the front steps of her house. The sun was setting, giving the sky an orange hue. Dré bumped his shoulder against hers playfully.

"Your parents are cool."

"I was so worried about them ganging up on you. I hope they weren't too hard on you."

Smiling, he played with the leaves on a nearby bush. "Nah, they were cool. Your parents were straightforward with me, and I have to say that's the way I like it."

"Did they ask you about the drugs?"

He stared out into the yard. "Yeah, they asked me. I can't say I blame them either. I'm bad news."

"Stop saying that! There's nothing wrong with you, Dré. Well . . . except for the drug thang."

"That's not an issue anymore," he reminded her. "I gave it up, remember?"

They made eye contact. "I hope you mean that, Dré."

Pushing a strand of her hair behind her ear, he leaned over and whispered in her ear. "No doubt, Denim. I wouldn't lie to you."

His warm breath on her ear caused her to giggle. He looked over his shoulder and kissed her quickly on the lips. Denim looked behind her to see if her parents were watching them. "What was that for?"

"Denim Mitchell, do I have to give you a reason every time I kiss you?" he asked. "If you need a reason, I can come up with a million right now."

She laughed. "Forget I asked."

"I'm glad you care enough about me to give me some tough love," Dré told her.

"I'm glad you listened to me," she said as she hugged her knees.

"Me too." They looked at the setting sun in silence.

"I forgot to tell you how fly you look. Those jeans are hitting you in all the right places."

"Thank you, Dré. You look hot yourself."

"Listen at you," he teased. "Thanks."

"You're welcome."

Dré smiled upon hearing that Denim thought he looked hot.

"So, do you think they're going to let us hang out?" she asked.

"I hope so, because I'm going crazy just sitting here next to you."

"You're full of it," she said, blushing.

He stood up and brushed the leaves off his lap. "I'm never full of it when it comes to you, Miss Mitchell."

Denim stood on the steps in front of him and folded her arms. He took a step up and towered over her.

"Well, I'd better be getting home. Dinner was da bomb. You're a great cook. I guess you'll let me know when or if your parents let you hang out, right?"

"Oh, without a doubt. Thanks for staying for dinner, and thank you so much for the portrait. It's beautiful!"

He shoved his hands in his pockets. "I'm glad you liked it. It was nothing."

"You have a gift, Dré."

"That's what everyone tells me," he replied humbly.

"Then embrace it and don't throw it away," she advised him.

Dré smiled and stared into Denim's beautiful eyes. "Don't worry; I won't."

He looked toward her front door and then took her hand. Denim held onto his hand as he pulled her up and led her out to the edge of the yard.

"Well, I guess I'll see you in school tomorrow."

"I guess so," she answered.

Once again, he leaned in without warning and kissed her quickly on the lips, then started walking down the sidewalk. He stopped a few feet down and turned to her.

"I like kissing you, Denim, and I hope I get the chance to kiss you a lot more."

Denim's face was hot, and chills ran down her arms. "Me too. See you later, Dré"

"Bye."

When Denim entered her house, her heart was pounding in her chest. Only Dré could make her body have that kind of reaction.

When she walked past the family room, her mom and dad called her in. She nervously sat down as her father stood and paced the floor. She hoped they didn't see Dré kiss her.

"Denim, your mother and I have decided to let you date Dré, but on a probationary basis. We believe he's sincere about you and his future, and we trust you and hope that you'll use the common sense God gave you. We were young once, and we remember what it was like to be a teenager. What I'm saying, Denim, is we're going to give you a chance. One slip-up, and that's it. Do you understand?"

Denim jumped out of her chair and hugged her mom and dad. "Yes, sir! Thank you so much! I won't let you down, and neither will Dré."

"I hope you mean it when you say you won't let us down," Valessa said. "We want to make sure you act responsibly. We've talked to you about drugs, sex, birth control, and diseases. If you feel like you are leaning toward the unthinkable, please come to me or your father. If Dré starts smoking again, you'd better walk away, and I mean it. Do you understand?"

"Yes, ma'am. Thank you," she said after hugging her parents once more. "I'm going to go clean up the kitchen now.

"Go ahead," Valessa instructed her.

Denim hurriedly cleaned up the kitchen and ran into her room so she could log onto her computer. She smiled as she typed Dré an e-mail message. When she was finished, she went over to her closet and picked out an outfit to wear to school. She wanted it to be an outfit Dré would never forget.

After laying out her clothes, she picked up her journal and made an entry:

> *Today was the first day of school and it was awesome. Where do I start? Well, that slut, Anika, tried to front me and push up on Dré, but I handled her with no problem. Then Dré kissed me in the hallway and it was heavenly. The boy can kiss! WHEW! I'm starting to have all types of emotions that I can't explain. Patrice said it was my hormones jumping off, but honestly, I don't have a clue what it is.*
>
> *I'm also thinking about redecorating my room. I'm over the girlie pastel colors. I want something more sophisticated and chic, like me. LOL!*
>
> *Now the good news . . . My parents are letting me go out with Dré!*
>
> *Life is good!*
>
> *Later,*
> *D*

Dré walked into his house and headed straight for his room. His dad walked out of the kitchen with a beer in his hand.

"Well, well, well. Guess who I just got a call from?"

"Who?" Dré asked.

"Samuel Mitchell called me and told me you asked him for permission to go out with his daughter. What's up with that?"

Dré sighed. "Nothing's up with it. I just feel like it's the right thing to do with a girl like Denim."

His father laughed and walked over to a nearby chair. "Where did this come from? You've known Denim all her life. What's changed?"

"You know I've always liked Denim," Dré answered. "Besides, we're older now."

His father took a sip of beer and set it down on the table. "Well, don't do anything stupid like get her pregnant or something. I can't be getting into any altercations with Mitchell. Do you understand me?"

"Yes, sir."

Dré turned to walk away, but his dad stopped him once more.

"By the way, Mitchell told me you assured him that you've given up weed. Is that a fact?"

"Yes, it's a fact, Daddy, and you should've never let me start in the first place," Dré replied in a challenging voice.

Nodding, his father agreed. "You're right. But there's

nothing I can do about that now. You have a brighter future than I had when I was your age. You're doing the right thing. I wish I had."

Dré walked over to his father and put his hand on his shoulder. "It's not too late for you either, Daddy."

His father looked up at him and shook his head. "Nah, it's a little too late for me, son, but you continue to do the right thang. Okay?"

Dré took his dad's beer off the table and poured it into his mother's flowers.

"It's never too late, Daddy."

Then Dré set the empty bottle on the table and walked out of the room. His dad was speechless.

Once in his room, Dré logged on to his computer under his screen name, Prime Time, and realized he had an e-mail message from Cocoa Princess, Denim's screen name. Opening it, he read the message:

Hey, Prime Time,

Thanks again for coming to dinner tonight. I care about you a lot, and I'm very happy to tell you that my parents said it was OK for us to hang out as long as you keep your word about drugs. So, I guess that means you'll get the chance to kiss me some more after all. I'll see you in school tomorrow.

See ya,
Cocoa Princess

Dré sat down and hit the reply button. His message read:

Hey, Cocoa Princess!
That's the best news I've heard in a long time. I can't wait to see you.

Sweet dreams,
Prime Time

Chapter Eight

Denim's sixteenth birthday rolled around, and instead of having a huge party, she just wanted an evening with her closest friends. When she made her way into the kitchen, her mom and dad were already at the table eating breakfast.

"Happy birthday, sweetheart!" her father yelled.

She walked over and gave him a kiss. "Thank you, Daddy."

Valessa stood and hugged her daughter. With tears in her eyes she said, "Happy birthday, Denim. I love you so much."

Denim hugged her mother lovingly. "I love you too, Mom. Thank you."

"So, Denim, are you ready for your birthday dinner party this weekend?" Valessa asked.

She sat down and took a sip of her orange juice. "It's

not really a dinner party, Mom. We're just having finger foods and drinks."

Samuel smiled and poured some cream in his coffee. "I can't believe you didn't want to have a big sweet sixteen party."

Denim picked up a piece of crispy bacon and took a bite. "I don't need all of that, Daddy. Having you guys, my three best friends, and a few other friends to celebrate with me is all I need. Well, you know I wish Antoine was here too."

Valessa put a spoonful of scrambled eggs onto her plate. "Your brother hated that he couldn't make it home for your birthday, but he sent you a present last week. We've kept it in our room so you wouldn't be tempted to open it. You can get it off our bed when you finish your breakfast."

"Oh my God! I can't wait to see what Antoine sent me."

Valessa buttered a biscuit and said, "It's a pretty big box, sweetie. I'm sure it's something to spoil you even more than he already has."

Denim picked up another piece of bacon and giggled. "My brother loves me and I love him. We spoil each other."

"We know that, Denim. You two are as thick as thieves," Samuel added as he reached into his pocket and held out a set of keys and smiled.

Denim's eyes widened. "Is that what I think it is, Daddy?"

"Yes, it is. Your car is ready to roll."

Denim grabbed the keys, jumped up out of her seat, and ran into the garage. She opened the door to her car and climbed inside. "Thank you! Thank you! Thank you!"

Valessa and Samuel followed her out into the garage. Samuel kicked the tires and said, "Denim, before you get excited, let's go over the rules one more time."

Denim put her hands on the steering wheel and decided to rap the rules instead of reciting them. "I must wear my seatbelt at all times; no drinking and driving, speeding, talking on the cell phone while driving. I'm not allowed to pick up hitchhikers; I have to keep at least a half tank of gas in the car at all times; only four people can be in the car at any given time, and keep the car clean. Whew! Did that cover everything?"

"Very funny, Denim Mitchell. That was a nice rendition of the rules, but you left out one very important rule."

She frowned and thought for a moment. "I can't remember anything else."

"Let me help you," Samuel volunteered as he leaned against the car. "No one drives your car but you, so make sure you don't let any of your friends behind the wheel of the car, including Dré."

Denim snapped her finger. "Oh yeah! I forgot about that one."

"That's one of the most important ones too," Valessa pointed out.

91

"Can I drive my car to school today?"

"It's your car, sweetie. You have your license and the keys. Just be careful, Denim."

"I will, Daddy."

"Good. Now go finish your breakfast so you won't be late to school."

Denim climbed out of the car and walked back into the house so she could finish her breakfast. It was going to be a great day, and she couldn't wait to put this milestone into her journal.

After breakfast, she raced upstairs and got the present Antoine sent her and ripped it open. Inside were a beautiful red leather purse and a lavender velour G-Unit warm-up suit with matching sneakers. In the bottom of the box was an envelope. When she pulled out the card and opened it, a hundred-dollar bill fell out on the bed. Tears welled up in her eyes as she read the loving card from her brother.

Denim immediately picked up the telephone and called Antoine. She cried the entire time she was on the telephone with him as she thanked him over and over for her birthday gifts. Before leaving for school, she pulled out her journal and jotted down a few notes.

Happy Birthday to me!! Yeah, today is my birth-day, and so far it's been unbelievable. Daddy finally finished restoring his Mustang for me, with a little help from Dré. Daddy even had it painted for me and it looks brand new. I'm driving my new silver bullet to school today and I can't wait for my friends to see it.

Oh! Antoine sent me a fly purse and outfit with the matching sneakers. G-Unit, of course. Last but not least, he stuck a C-note in my birthday card. I have the best brother in the world!!

I'm excited about my dinner party with my friends this weekend. Mom helped me plan the menu, and as my present, she's taking care of all the catering. It's not going to be anything fancy, just friends hanging out, playing cards, dancing, and having a great time. I'm going to keep my fingers crossed that I'll get something extra special from Dré.

Well, I have to run before I'm late for school. Holla!

The Birthday Girl,
D

Denim drove her Mustang to school and surprised all her friends.

The next few days, Denim hung out with her friends at school, and before she realized it, the weekend had arrived. Dré asked her to go with him to the first high school football game. All their friends would be there, as well as most of the student body.

Valessa was reluctant about Denim riding with Dré, but Samuel assured her they would have to start giving her some freedom if they were allowing her to date and to drive. Valessa remembered the first night they let Antoine drive. Her stomach was in knots that night as well. She knew she wouldn't rest until Denim was safely back at home.

When Dré picked her up, Samuel had a very long talk with him.

"Dré, I want to reiterate to you that Denim's curfew is midnight and not a minute later. Be careful. No drinking or anything else—and I don't have to tell you what I'm talking about."

Dré nodded. "You don't have to worry about that, Mr. Mitchell."

"Drive safely, and if you have any car problems or any issues at all, I want you to call me right away. Do you understand?"

"Yes, sir," Dré answered as he sat patiently in the Mitchells' family room.

Within minutes, Denim appeared with a huge smile on her face. Samuel turned to her and frowned. Denim was dressed a little older than he preferred, but he held his tongue this time. She had on a snug pair of denim capri pants with a matching jacket that barely covered her midsection and a pair of sandals with a slight heel. Samuel looked over at Valessa and she read his mind, but winked at him to tell him everything was OK.

"Denim, keep your cell phone on at all times," Valessa instructed her.

Rolling her eyes, she let out a sigh. "I will, Mom." She

kissed her dad's cheek. "Good-bye, Daddy. I'll see you guys after the game."

Standing in the doorway, Samuel and Valessa watched the two teens as they climbed into Dré's car and pulled away from the curb. Valessa turned to Samuel. "My stomach is in knots. I hope we're doing the right thing, Samuel."

He kissed her on the forehead and led her back into the house.

"We knew this day would eventually come. I'm sure everything will be okay."

She hugged his waist. "I hope you're right."

At the game, their friends who had been waiting for them to arrive greeted Denim and Dré. They all sat together in the bleachers, but Dré made sure Denim stayed close by his side. He wasn't ashamed to show his affection to her. When he wasn't hugging her waist, he was holding her hand. Denim noticed the unwelcome glares from Anika and her friends and so did Dré, but he didn't care.

"Forget about them, Denim."

"You're right," she replied as she raised her hand to get the attention of a concession stand attendant. "Hot dog!"

The attendant walked over to them. She looked over at Dré and asked, "Would you like one?"

"Yes, but I'm buying."

Denim pulled out her money. "Not this time. I got it."

"Look at you. That birthday money is burning in your

pocket, huh?" he teased. "Seriously though, next time it's my treat. Okay, Cocoa Princess?"

She paid the attendant and gave Dré a quick kiss on the lips. "Whatever you say, Prime Time."

He stared at her with a smile on his face. Denim looked over at him and blushed. "Why are you staring at me?"

Dré put his arm around her waist. "I'm sure you're wondering why I haven't given you my gift yet."

Denim replied, "Not really."

"Liar," he teased again. "Anyway, I have your gift, but I wanted to give it to you when we were alone."

This bit of information intrigued her. "What is it? Where is it?"

"You'll get it in due time. Patience, babe."

Excited, Denim started searching Dré's pockets. He laughed and said, "All right, you better be careful where you put your hands. You know I'm sensitive to your touch."

Denim immediately stopped searching him. "You're going to leave me in suspense all night, aren't you?"

"Dré took a bite of his hot dog and looked her in the eyes. "Not all night. You'll get it soon enough."

She swallowed the lump in her throat. Denim had no idea what Dré was up to, but she realized she wasn't going to get any information out of him now. To try to get her mind off her birthday gift, she joined her friends in cheering for their football team. Occasionally Dré would lean over and kiss Denim. His cologne filled her nostrils with the most sensual and pleasant scent, and it was one that she wouldn't soon forget.

The game ended with their team victorious. It was only ten o'clock, so the group headed to a local hamburger joint to eat and hang out. Dré kept a close eye on his watch because he didn't want to do anything to ruin his chances to take Denim out again.

"It's getting late, Denim. We'd better get going," Dré said once he noticed that Denim had finished her fries.

Laughing, Denim stood and sipped the last of her soda. "I guess you're right. Well, people, we're out! We'll see you guys later."

In unison, their friends said good-bye.

"Don't you two do anything I wouldn't do," Patrice added sarcastically. Laughing, Dré opened up the car door for Denim so she could get inside.

Before closing the door, Denim said, "Very funny, Patrice."

Halfway home, Dré looked over at Denim and smiled. "I had fun tonight."

"Me too," Denim answered while blushing.

"Are you ready for your gift?" he asked as he pulled over and parked in downtown Freedman.

"I guess," she replied.

"Let's go over to the fountain in the square," Dré requested as he climbed out of the car.

Denim opened her car door before Dré could walk around to open it. He held out his hand and took hers into his. They walked hand in hand across the street to the large fountain that sat in the middle of downtown. It had been a fixture in Freedman for over fifty years, and was a meeting point for senior citizens during the day and teens at night. Thankfully, because of the football game, their fellow teens found somewhere else to hang out tonight.

"I love the sound of water," Denim pointed out as she sat down and dipped her hand into the cool water.

Dré stood in front of her with a huge smile on his face. "Yeah, it's cool. Not a lot of people out here tonight."

Denim patted the spot next to her and said, "Come and sit down with me, Prime Time."

He took his seat next to Denim in silence. She tilted her head and studied him. If she didn't know better, she would think Dré was nervous. "Why are you so quiet?" she asked.

Dré pulled a small red box with a white bow out of his pocket and set it in Denim's lap. "What's this?"

"Open it and see," Dré replied softly. Denim picked up the small velvet box, slowly opened it, and froze.

"Dré, it's beautiful."

He smiled and took the box out of her hand. Inside was a ring with a small princess cut diamond on it. Dré placed it on her left hand and then kissed it.

"I'm glad you like it. I've been saving up for it. Happy birthday, baby."

Denim cupped Dré's face and kissed him slowly on the lips. "I love my ring and I love you."

"I love you too, and I'm glad you like the ring. I wish it could've been more."

Denim shook her head. "No, it's perfect, and you really didn't have to."

"I know I didn't have to. I wanted to because I needed to show you how much you mean to me. I'm not playing games with you, Denim. I want us to be official."

"Wow, Dré! I don't know what to say."

He smiled. "You've said all I need to hear. Now come on, so I can get you home before you miss curfew."

Denim stood. She couldn't take her eyes off her ring. Dré took her other hand and together, they ran across the street to his car. Seconds later, they were on their way to Denim's house.

Chapter Nine

Dré pulled into Denim's driveway and turned off the engine. They sat there in silence for a moment before Denim looked at her ring once more. "I still can't believe it."

"Believe it. I don't know why you're so surprised. You know how l feel about you."

Denim looked at her watch. She had about fifteen minutes left before her curfew. Dré also noticed the time. "I'd better walk you to the door."

He got out of the car and walked around to open her door. When she got out, he wrapped his arms around her waist and hugged her tightly. Denim hugged him back, closing her eyes. She buried her face in his chest and savored the warmth of his body.

"We'd better pull up before your dad comes out here with his nine millimeter."

Denim giggled loudly. "Daddy wouldn't do that."

"Oh, yes he would, and I can't say I blame him. You're so fine, Denim. I know how I feel when other guys look at you, so I can't imagine the stress your dad is going through seeing you with me."

They laughed together as they walked up the sidewalk to her porch. When they reached the steps, Denim stepped up on two of them so she could be eye level with him. She wrapped her arms around his neck and stared up into his handsome face.

"Well, aren't you going to kiss me good night?"

Grinning, he pulled her closer and kissed her gently on her soft, rose-colored lips. Denim savored the feel of his tall, muscular body against hers. Denim's stomach fluttered and a warm sensation engulfed her body. Dré finally pulled away.

"Whew, Cocoa Princess!"

"Ditto that, Prime Time, and thank you again for my beautiful ring. I'll never take it off. This has been the best birthday ever. Tomorrow night will be even better when you guys come over for my party."

"I can't wait. Good night, babe," he said softly.

"Good night, Dré."

Denim hurried upstairs after giving her dad a good night hug. Entering her room, she immediately pulled out her diary and began to write:

Tonight was my first date with Dré and the night of our big football game. Of course we won, and everybody who's anybody was there. After the game, we all met up for burgers at Jenk's Grill.

That hoochie Anika was there, and if she had given me one wrong look, I was going to snatch that weave right out of her head. Luckily for her she kept her distance.

Patrice and DeMario couldn't keep their hands off each other, which was a little disgusting. I'm not hating, but there's a time and place for everything.

It was also a night I'll never forget. Dré and I became official. He gave me a beautiful ring for my birthday, and we shared some of the sweetest kisses before he drove me home.

I'm a little sleepy now, so I'm going to shower, stare at my ring a little more and then go to sleep. I can't wait to see Dré tomorrow.

Later,
D

When Dré returned home, he found his father was waiting up for him. Dré walked into their family room and leaned against the doorframe. "You're not waiting up for me, are you?"

His father chuckled as he picked up the remote and changed the station on the TV. "No, but there is something I want to talk to you about."

Dré sat down on the sofa and waited for his father to speak. He watched him as he lit a cigarette and blew a circular puff of smoke out of his mouth. "Son, I've been doing a lot of thinking. You've made it clear how you feel about my business dealings, and it's cool. Everyone has a talent, and mine happens to be with numbers. I'm not saying it's right, but it's what I know. The numbers game has been around long before me."

"But the lottery is legal now, so why do you still have to do it?" Dré asked.

"Old schoolers don't accept change that much. They like the way things have been, and it's never going to change. Dré, let's change the subject.

"Your mother and me had a long talk, and I want you to stay focused and keep your head in the books. I have no doubt that you're going to make a name for yourself, and I want you to know that I'm proud of you and I'm sorry I haven't been able to make it to as many games as I've wanted to. I'm going to try and do better, son, and one day I'm going to make you proud of your old man. You'll see."

Dré looked at his father curiously because he wasn't sure if he was going to stand by his word. His mother did have a huge influence over his father, though, and if she had anything to do with it, she would make sure he did.

Dré stood and said, "Thanks, Daddy."

"Before you go to bed, say good night to your mother," his father instructed before lighting another cigarette.

Dré walked past his father and answered, "I will. Good night, Daddy."

The night of Denim's birthday party had finally arrived, and she couldn't wait to see her friends. Downstairs, Valessa made sure that all the food Denim had requested was set up as well as the decorations. She had trays of chicken salad sandwiches, hot wings, fruits and vegetables, as well as a variety of cheeses and crackers. There were also bowls of chips and dip and a punch-bowl full of fruit punch. The two-tier pink birthday cake was covered in buttercream and fondant icing with an array of edible flowers arranged in a decorative and inviting pattern. On top of it were candles in the shape of the number sixteen. It made a beautiful centerpiece to the entire table.

Upstairs, Denim was putting the finishing touches on her makeup. She was dressed in a long pink skirt with a matching halter top. Her sandals accented her attire, and so did the diamond teardrop earrings her mother let her borrow.

"Denim, you'd better hurry up! Your guests will be here in a second!" Valessa yelled from downstairs.

She stood and said, "I'm coming, Mom." Before leaving her room, she glanced down at the ring on her finger and at her appearance in the mirror one more time.

Tears welled up in Valessa's eyes when Denim entered the room.

"Everything is so pretty. Thank you!" Denim walked over and hugged her mother.

"You're welcome, sweetheart."

Denim stole a piece of cheese off the tray and stuck it in her mouth. "Are you sure you and Daddy have to stay here while my party's going on?"

Valessa sighed. "Denim, you're growing up, but we're not ready to let you have a party completely unsupervised. Your father and I will be out in the backyard with the Moores from next door. This way we can keep an eye on things and give you guys some privacy at the same time."

"I guess that will be okay, but don't let Daddy and Mr. Moore keep coming into the house. You know how silly they get when they're together."

Valessa laughed. Denim was right about one thing. When Samuel and Justin got together, they did act like a couple of college boys. She held both of Denim's hands. "I'll do what I can, Denim."

"Thank you, Mom."

Valessa looked down at Denim's hand and frowned. "What is this?"

Denim bit her lip and said, "Oh, it's just a ring Dré gave me for my birthday."

Valessa inspected it closer. "It's pretty and it looks expensive. I don't know about you accepting such a suggestive gift from Dré."

Denim pulled away and said, "It's just a ring. It's not like it's an engagement ring or anything. Besides, we're going out, so it's not unusual for a girl my age to get a ring from her boyfriend."

Valessa shuffled a couple of the trays on the table and said, "I know, Denim, but that's no bubblegum ring."

Denim walked over and touched her mother's arm to comfort her. "It's okay. You don't have to worry. We're not going to run off to Vegas and get married or anything."

Valessa turned and said, "That's not funny, Denim."

Denim giggled upon seeing her mother's reaction, and at that moment, the doorbell rang. "They're here!"

The night was full of fun and laughter. Denim and her friends danced, ate, played cards and trivia games, and just hung out and enjoyed each other's company. Later, Denim opened her gifts and was excited to receive so many beautiful items from her friends. She was especially happy that her parents kept their distance and stayed in the backyard with their neighbors. Denim did check on them at one point when she went to get more ice for her guests. She found them enjoying each other's company, drinking wine and playing bid whist. It was a glorious birthday party, and Denim would never forget it for the rest of her life.

When the party was over, Denim's friends stayed to help her clean up. Dré was the last one to leave, and before he left, he made sure he gave her a kiss that set off a whirlwind of explosives and set her soul on fire.

Before going to bed, she made a brief recording in her journal:

I'm exhausted, but in a good way. My party was a hit, and all my friends had a great time. Thanks to Mom and Daddy, the food was on point, and they allowed me to have the house to myself— well, sort of. Mom tried to freak out over my ring, but she's cool now.

Dré looked so fine tonight. When he walked

through the door, I thought I was going to pass out. We danced, and when he held me in his arms, I melted.

DeMario and Patrice got into an argument over a text message he got, but Dré, being the great guy he is, made them squash it. Before the night was over, Patrice and DeMario were back in love again. They're so stupid and made for each other.

Anyway, I'm headed to bed and anxious to wake up so I can talk to Dré.

Later,
D

Weeks had passed since Denim's birthday, and the leaves on the trees had turned from green to red and orange. Dré and Denim were continuing to enjoy their relationship, which seemed to heat up as each day passed. They shared only one class together, which meant going out on the weekend was even more special. Patrice and DeMario were still together, which was amazing in itself, since they seemed to fight most of the time. Oddly enough, when they weren't fighting, they couldn't keep their hands off each other. This made their dates even more fun because the four of them would often double date.

Thanksgiving was approaching, and autumn was definitely in the air. Denim couldn't wait for Christmas break because she planned to get something very special for Dré. She was also looking forward to Antoine coming home for Thanksgiving, so they could spend some time together.

But on this day when she walked through the door, her world came crashing down on her. She found her mom and dad waiting silently in the family room.

"Denim, could you come in here, please?" her father called out to her.

She realized her dad's voice was strained, and she noticed him pacing the floor when she entered the room. This was never a good sign. Denim walked farther into the room and spoke reluctantly.

"Yes, sir?"

Samuel picked up a clear plastic bag, and when Denim saw what it was, she nearly fainted.

"Denim, what the hell is this? And don't you lie to me!"

Inside the bag was the bloodstained blouse and bra she had on the night of the shooting at Dré's birthday party. Stuttering, she tried to explain, but Valessa immediately put her hand up to cut her off.

"Denim! Before lies start falling out of your mouth, we already know you were at Dré's party the night of that shooting because we saw a picture someone took, and you were in the background with this blouse on. What we don't know is how in the hell did your clothes get blood all over them?"

Sweat had now broken out on Denim's brow. "Mom, I can explain."

Samuel yelled at her, which is something he rarely did. "Explain what, Denim? That you snuck out of this house in the middle of the night and damn near got yourself killed?"

"Daddy, I'm sorry. I was only gone for a minute. I promise."

Her father stalked toward her and shoved the plastic bag in her face. "I want to know right now how your clothes ended up in police possession!"

Denim wasn't used to lying, but she didn't want to get Dré into trouble either. This was her war, and she needed to fight the battle alone.

"When I heard gunshots, I started running, and I guess I must've fallen somewhere near the boy who got shot."

Valessa stood and grabbed the plastic bag out of Samuel's hand. "So you mean to tell me that you came home topless?"

"No, ma'am. Dré gave me his shirt to put on, and then he walked me home."

Samuel sighed. "So Dré is involved in this?" he asked.

"No, Daddy! Dré was the one who got me out of there and back home safely."

Samuel's eyes were as red as she had ever seen them. A large vein was pulsating in his neck, which let her know he was beyond angry. "Well, you can forget about Dré and everything else, as far as I'm concerned. You also better get used to looking at the four walls in your room because that's all you're going to see for a long time. Give me the keys to your car."

Tears dropped from Denim's eyes as she reached inside her purse and handed her father the keys to her car. "I'm sorry, Daddy."

"Not another word, Denim!"

Her parents had been angry before, but never this angry. She didn't understand how they couldn't see her side to the story, but then again, she did sneak out of the house. All three of them stood there in silence for a moment before Samuel spoke again.

"Denim, how do you think it made me and your mother feel to open the door and find a detective standing there with our daughter's bloodstained clothes? They thought you had been shot too."

Denim was speechless. She had no words in her defense. What she worried about most was whether her parents were going to fault Dré in all of this.

"I'm sorry I disappointed you," she apologized.

Samuel was still furious and didn't respond to her apology. Instead, he pointed toward the doorway. "Denim, don't think for one minute you're too old to get a beat down. Go to your room. Now!"

Denim ran to her room, crying hysterically, and quickly turned on her computer. She knew she couldn't risk making a telephone call, so an e-mail to Dré was the next best thing. When she finished typing the e-mail, she quickly turned off her computer and lay across her bed, broken-hearted. She pulled out her journal and recorded an entry:

Today was a good day until I came home from school. My parents found out I snuck out of the house to go to Dré's party, and to say they are pissed is an understatement. 5-0 showed up at the door with my bloody clothes. They tracked me down from pictures someone took at the party, and actually thought I had been shot too. Daddy took my car from me, and I'll probably be grounded until I'm old and gray. I know they're going to be angry for a long time, but I feel like they created the situation. They've made me feel like a prisoner and I had to break out. I'm sixteen, for God's sake, not six!

Pray for me because I don't know if they'll ever let me see Dré again!

Heartbroken,
D

Downstairs, Valessa threw the plastic bag with Denim's clothes in it onto the table.

"Samuel, that is *your daughter* upstairs. What made her think she could sneak out of this house without us finding out about it?"

He sat down and put his head in his hands. "She has lost her damn mind. I know that for sure. I almost got sick when I saw that blouse. Does she know how serious what she did is? One stray bullet and it would have been all over."

Valessa crossed the room and sat next to her husband. She put her arm around him to comfort him.

"Sweetheart, I feel just as sick as you do about this. Denim's going to have to realize there are consequences to her careless actions. I was hoping she wouldn't try some of the stunts her friends are probably doing. We're going to have to keep a close eye on her without completely shutting her down. I don't want her to stop communicating with us altogether."

"She violated our rules the moment she snuck out of this house. She is not to drive her car, get on the telephone, computer, or anything else until I say so. She can also forget about dating until she's thirty! I want her in this house after school."

Valessa turned Samuel's face so they were eye to eye.

"Samuel, I'm just as angry as you are, but let's calm down for a moment. First we need to thank God that Denim didn't get hurt or killed. Don't you agree?"

"Being calm is the last thing on my mind right now," Samuel said while shaking his head. "I just can't believe my baby girl did this."

Valessa smiled. "She's not a baby girl anymore, and that's part of her problem. She's growing up on us, and her hormones are raging. I'm so thankful things didn't turn out differently. We could be planning her funeral right now, but we're not. We have to be thankful for that."

"You're right, but she's still grounded until she graduates college. You don't know how badly I wish we could turn back the hands of time and keep her a little girl. You know?"

"I know, Samuel," Valessa agreed as she laid her head on his shoulder.

"I think it would be a good idea to make Denim volunteer in the trauma rehabilitation center so she can see what people who've been shot have to go through. They have plenty of gunshot victims down there."

"Sounds like a great idea. Now, go talk to your daughter."

He stood up and said, "I think that's a good idea."

Samuel left the room and headed upstairs to reassure Denim that he loved her in spite of her disobedience.

Chapter Ten

Dré came in from his part-time job at the local music store and threw his keys on the dresser. He turned on his computer and noticed a message from the Cocoa Princess. Smiling, he decided to read the message before taking his shower. His smile quickly left his face when he read the e-mail.

Dré,

I got busted! My parents found out I was at your party. The police showed up with my bloody clothes in a bag. I told them you only helped me get home, not that you helped me sneak out. I wanted to warn you because they might try to call or come over to talk to you and your parents. They are so pissed! I'm grounded forever, so I'll only be able to see you at school for a while. They took my car, and they might even take my computer from me, so if you don't get an e-mail from me, you'll know why. Let Patrice know what happened. I love you.

Cocoa Princess

Dré knew he was in serious trouble. Denim never called him by his real name when they chatted. He turned off the computer and walked into the kitchen to tell his mom the news. He knew she would be cool if Denim's parents called or came by.

Another week had passed since Denim was officially grounded, and she was thankful that her parents decided not to take her computer from her. It was her only line of communication with the outside world once she got home from school. Besides, she needed it for homework assignments. She wasn't allowed to have company, though, so Patrice was banned from the house indefinitely.

As she sat there writing her term paper, she couldn't help but go online for a second. Her mailbox had two messages waiting on her. One e-mail was from Patrice, who used the screen name Chocolate Diva, and the other was from Prime Time. She read Patrice's e-mail first because she wanted to save Dré's for last. Patrice talked about school, homework, and DeMario. Denim quickly responded so she could move on to Dré's message. She opened it with a smile on her face.

Hey, Cocoa Princess,

*Just wanted to pop in and let you know I miss
you. The few moments we see each other at school
is killing me. I hope your old man lets you out of
the joint soon. I'm on my way to work and can't
wait to see you in class tomorrow. Hang in there,
babe, and be cool.*

*Love Ya,
Prime Time*

Denim pushed the reply button.

Hey, Prime Time!

*If it wasn't for your e-mails, I don't know what
I would do. I miss you too. I'm going crazy here
on lockdown. My parents haven't given any sign
of releasing me from this prison anytime soon.*

*I talked to Antoine today. He told me to hang in
there too. I'll be happy when he comes home.
Maybe it'll take some attention off of me. Anyway, I can't wait to see you.*

*Love You!
Cocoa Princess*

After logging off the computer, Denim picked up her
journal and made a quick entry:

*I haven't had anything exciting to report in
such a long time because I'm so sad. I'm still on*

lockdown and it's killing me. I guess that was the purpose, though. Daddy can't seem to make eye contact with me at times. I know I really hurt him. Mom is taking everything in stride. Actually, I think she's enjoying the fact that I'm not able to see Dré. Now that I've had a chance to look back on things, I realize that sneaking out of the house was stupid. That bullet could've killed me or Dré. Life is too short, and I'll do whatever I can to make it up to my parents.

Later,
D

Three and a half weeks elapsed, and Denim was really starting to feel the pressure of being grounded. She missed hanging out with Patrice and her other friends, but she missed Dré the most. She was just getting used to his warm hugs and delicious kisses.

On this particular morning before school, her Dad walked in and gave her a gift she wasn't expecting.

"Denim, your mom and I decided that we're going to lift your punishment for now, but you're still on probation. We've also decided that since you have transportation now, as part of your probation, you'll be working at the hospital as a volunteer."

Denim was confused. "A volunteer at the hospital? Doing what, Daddy?"

"Honey, we want you to work in the physical rehabilitation center in the trauma unit. We want you to see what the result can be to a bad situation like what you got caught up in. Maybe it'll help you think twice about sneaking out of the house again."

Denim knew she couldn't defy her father. "Okay, Daddy. How long will I be on probation?"

He folded his arms and leaned against her door. "That depends on you, sweetheart. What you did really hurt us. You're going to have to regain our trust, and it's not going to happen overnight."

Sighing, Denim lowered her head. "Can I drive my car?"

"Yes, but only to school and work. Other than that you need our approval."

"Am I allowed to go out with Dré?"

"That's a tough question, especially after what happened at his party."

"But, Daddy, Dré was the one who got me out safely. He made sure I made it home without getting hurt. Daddy, Dré would never let anything happen to me."

"Your judgment is what scares us, Denim. You're growing up and there's not a lot we can do to prevent it. Life is about choices. We know you're going to make mistakes, but we want you to do everything within your power to make the right choices in life. Hopefully, by you working at the hospital, it'll drive our point home."

She walked over and hugged her dad's waist.

"I understand, and I'm sorry I disappointed you. I promise I'll never do anything like that again."

He hugged her lovingly. "Just use some common sense, Denim. Okay?"

She stepped away and wiped some stray tears from her eyes. "I will, Daddy."

"I know. Now go eat breakfast so you can get to school."

"So, can I still date Dré or not, Daddy?"

"Don't push me, Denim. I'll have to talk to your mother about it and get back with you."

She blew him a kiss. "I love you, Daddy. Have a good day at work."

He waved her off and said, "Yeah, yeah, yeah. Have a good day at school."

During lunchtime in the school cafeteria, Denim announced to her friends that she was officially off punishment, but on indefinite probation. Dré was the one most interested in the news, of course. He took a bite of his sandwich and winked at her.

"Does this mean you can go to the football game with me on Friday?" he asked.

Denim shrugged her shoulders. "I don't know, Dré. I have to start working at the hospital as part of my punishment for sneaking out of the house."

"For real?" Dré asked.

She took a sip of her apple juice and said, "Yes. So I don't know how much extra time I'm going to have to hang out with you guys."

"It's cool. You know I have a job too," Dré said.

DeMario added, "Me too."

"Yeah, but at least you guys are getting paid for your time. My parents are making me volunteer. That's double torture." Denim rolled her eyes.

Patrice frowned and asked, "I need a job. When do you have to start, Denim?"

"I don't know. I'll have to ask my mom and dad. You know they're not two seconds off me right now, and I can't mess this up."

Dré leaned over and kissed her on the corner of her soft lips.

"Don't worry about it, babe. Do what they tell you to do. I'll come over and ask them myself if you can go to the game with me. By the way, I like your sexy outfit."

"Thanks, Dré," she replied with a smile. Dré always made it a point to compliment her on her attire. Today she had on a pair of House of Deréon jeans, a burnt orange sweater, and heels.

"You're welcome. You know I love complimenting my baby."

Denim blushed. "Are you sure about facing my parents after what happened?"

He fed her a piece of his apple pie. "I'm positive, so let me take care of it. I'd eventually have to face them anyway. Now is as good a time as any."

Smiling with approval, she was obviously impressed with his courage. Hopefully, her parents would be just as impressed.

At the end of the day, Denim walked out into the parking lot with Patrice. Dré blew his horn and yelled at the pair.

"You ladies want to go somewhere and get something to eat?"

"Well?" Patrice asked Denim.

Denim unlocked her car so they could put their books and other items into the car. "Go right ahead, Patrice. I can't go anywhere but school and work without my parents' permission while I'm on probation."

"Oh yeah, my bad," Patrice replied as she twirled a strand of her braids around her finger.

"Come on," Denim said, sighing as they walked over to Dré's car. DeMario sat inside, fumbling with the CD player. Dré exited the car and leaned against the door, grinning while Patrice talked to DeMario.

"Wipe that grin off your face, Prime Time. You know I have to go straight home from school or work unless I have my parents' permission."

"I know. I was just testing you, Cocoa Princess."

"Sure you were."

They laughed together, and then Dré pulled her closer. He whispered in her ear.

"If your parents let you go to the game Friday night, I have something very special planned for us."

"Really?"

He touched her cheek and caressed it. "Really. I think you're really going to like it too," he said with a hint of sensuality.

Dré's announcement sent chills down her spine.

At that second, Patrice yelled for Denim, snapping her out of her trance. "Denim, your cell phone is ring-ing." Before she could turn away, Dré grabbed her by the waist and gave her a slow, sensual kiss. It felt wonderful and new, since a month had passed since their last kiss. This time was different because he French kissed her tenderly, startling her. Seeing her surprise, he released her.

"I'll see you later," he said.

Clearing her throat, she took a step back. "Okay. I have to go."

"A'ight. Later, babe."

"Bye!" she yelled as hurried back to her car so she could answer her cell phone. By the time she got there, it had stopped. Denim looked at the caller ID and saw that it was Antoine.

"That was Antoine. I'll call him back after I get home," she told Patrice.

"When you talk to Antoine, tell him I still love him."

Denim rolled her eyes as she checked her phone to make sure she didn't miss any other calls.

"Speaking of love, you and Dré was getting it on so hard that you didn't even hear your cell ringing," Patrice pointed out.

"I know. Girl, he French kissed me."

"For real?"

"Uh-huh," Denim answered with a big smile.

"That's old news and the only way I kiss DeMario."

Denim climbed behind the steering wheel and said, "You're such a freak, Patrice."

At home, Denim called Antoine back before starting on her homework. He was just checking in on her and asking her about her day, as usual. Afterward, she hurriedly worked through her homework because she wanted to be finished when Dré showed up to talk to her parents.

As she finished up her homework, Valessa came to her room and sat down. Denim looked up from her paper and said, "Hi, Mom."

"Hi, Denim. Could you stop working on your homework for a second?"

"Yes, ma'am."

"I just came in to let you know that I decided to make you an appointment at my gynecologist for after school tomorrow."

"Why, Mom?"

Valessa patted the space on the bed next to her. Denim sat next to her and smiled.

She put her arm around Denim's shoulders. "You're a young woman now, Denim, and I want to teach you how to take care of your body. You've had your cycle for a couple of years now, and while I pray you're not sexually active, you might have questions about it. Sweetheart, I want you to be able to talk to me about *anything*, but if for some reason you don't feel comfortable talking to me, I want you to get the facts from a professional. Okay?"

Denim swallowed hard before responding to her mother. "Would you be upset with me if I wanted to get birth control pills?"

Valessa put her hand over her heart and let out a breath. She was startled by Denim's request, but she held her composure. "Denim, I'm not a fan of your request. In fact, you nearly gave me a heart attack, but I'd rather you have them before you're sexually active, than not have them if and when that moment comes. Just remember, birth control pills only prevent pregnancy. You have to take other measures to protect yourself from diseases. Okay?"

"I know, Mom. They teach us about our bodies in health class at school," she revealed. She hugged her mother's waist to comfort her. "You don't have to worry, because I'm not doing anything with anybody."

Holding Denim made Valessa realize that it wasn't that long ago that she held her in her arms as a newborn. She caressed Denim's back and said, "That's comforting to know, Denim."

"How old were you when you did it for the first time?"

Denim's next question definitely caught Valessa off guard. She wanted to be truthful with her daughter, but she didn't want her answer to encourage her to do something she wasn't emotionally ready for. After thinking about Denim's question for a moment, Valessa gave her the best answer she could.

"Well, Denim, what I did when I was your age is irrelevant to you. I want you to map your own future on your own time. What I'm saying, sweetheart, is that I don't want you to gauge your life by the things I did. You need to make your decisions by the life you're leading, not the one I've already lived. Do you understand?"

Valessa's response wasn't the answer Denim was looking for, yet it made a lot of sense.

Denim made her way back over to her desk and sat down. She sighed and said, "I understand."

"Denim, I also want you to be aware that a lot of boys will tell you what you want to hear, just so they can get what they want from you. You have to be very protective of your body and treat it like a temple. If you don't respect or protect it, no one else will. Understand?"

"Yes, ma'am."

"Good. Now, Denim, tomorrow if you want birth control pills or any other contraceptive, I support you. This doesn't mean I'm giving you permission to have sex. It just means I'm giving you ammunition to protect yourself."

Denim hugged her mother's neck. "Thank you, Mom."

Relieved, Valessa stood to leave her daughter's room. "Before I go, I wanted to tell you that we've arranged for you to work at the hospital two weekends out of the month."

For a high school student that was eternity.

"Two weekends?"

With a raised brow, Valessa folded her arms. "And the problem is?"

Denim lowered her head. Even though she hated giving up her weekends, she had to accept her sentence. It could be worse. She could still be on punishment and unable to see Dré.

"There's no problem. When do I start?"

"Next weekend. This is for your own good, Denim. It's teaching you a lesson, you'll be helping people, and it's a community service. You might not see it this way, but by volunteering, it's something you can put on your résumé."

"Yes, ma'am," Denim answered.

"Good. Dinner will be ready in ten minutes," she said.

"Okay. I'll be down in a minute."

Closing the door, Valessa backed out of Denim's room. "Don't take too long," she yelled through the door.

"I won't."

Smiling, Denim pulled out her journal once again.

I'm off punishment, thank God! Unfortunately, I'm on probation, and part of my probation is that I'm going to have to volunteer at the hospital and work with trauma patients. Daddy said he was doing it so I could understand the conse-quences of what could've happened to me at Dré's party.

On another note, I had an unexpected victory with Mom. She's going to take me to the doctor to-morrow so I can get birth control pills. Yippeee! I'm excited but a little nervous too. I don't know what to expect, but I'm sure whatever happens will be worth it in the end.

Later,
D

Chapter Eleven

Valessa leaned against the door and did her best to calm her rapidly beating heart. Walking back inside the kitchen, Samuel looked up and saw Valessa's distress.

"What's wrong, sweetheart?"

Sitting down at the table, she took a sip of iced tea. "I'm taking Denim to my gynecologist tomorrow. She wants birth control pills."

Samuel was speechless. He set the casserole down on the countertop without speaking and walked out into the garage. Valessa thought he was going out for only a second. After several minutes passed, she looked out the window to find him sitting in the backyard. Valessa wanted to run down the street screaming, but she couldn't. She had to be there for her daughter. No matter how uncomfortable the subject made her feel, the day they dreaded had arrived.

* * *

Samuel did come in for dinner, but with a heavy heart. Denim picked up on his solemn mood. Puzzled, she looked at him.

"Daddy, are you okay?"

Raising his fork to his mouth, he paused. "I'm okay, baby. I just have some things on my mind."

When he looked across the table, he visualized Denim at age six, not sixteen. Tears formed in his eyes as he realized she was a young woman. He set his fork down and smiled.

"Daddy, if you don't mind, can you show me the basic mechanics on my car? I need to learn a little something about cars since I have one now."

"You're right, Denim. If you're going to be driving a car, you do need to know how to take care of it."

Denim got up from the table, walked over to Samuel, and hugged his neck. "I love you, Daddy."

He kissed her cheek and said, "I love you, too, baby."

"So, do you want to start showing me stuff about the car tonight, Daddy?"

"If you want to."

"I have to do the dishes first."

"That'll be fine. I'll be waiting," Samuel said as he took the last bite of his dinner.

He removed his plate from the table. Valessa could feel his sadness, but she knew somehow they would get through Denim's teenage years together. Samuel kissed Valessa on the lips and picked up his car keys.

"I'm getting ready to run to the auto supply store to pick up a few items. I'll be back in a minute."

"Okay, babe. Be careful."

"I will," he replied as he walked out of the dining room and to the front door. When he opened the door, he found Dré standing there with a big smile on his face.

"Good evening, Mr. Samuel. Hello, Mrs. Valessa. I didn't mean to interrupt your dinner."

Samuel frowned. All of a sudden, Dré was looking much older than he had been. In fact, he was looking like a grown man, and he was there to see Samuel's daughter.

Valessa waved him in. "We're just finishing up, Dré. Come on in."

Dré noticed Denim sitting at the table, and a huge smile appeared on his face. Denim smiled back at him, but before he could say anything to her, Samuel intervened.

"He's not coming in right now. He's going with me."

Samuel backed Dré onto the porch and closed the door behind them. He pointed at him and said, "You, come with me."

"Yes, sir," Dré replied as he followed Samuel over to his car. Valessa had no idea what Samuel was about to say or do to Dré, but whatever it was, she hoped it would relieve some of the anxiety her husband was experiencing.

* * *

On the ride to the auto supply store, Samuel and Dré rode in silence. Dré could feel the tension between them, so he decided to break the silence.

"Mr. Samuel, will it be okay with you and Mrs. Valessa if I take Denim to the football game this Friday night?"

Turning to look at Dré, Samuel frowned. "You know, Dré, I was sixteen once, and I know how it feels when your hormones are bouncing off the wall. I wasn't born yesterday, and I know Denim didn't sneak out of the house all by herself. I also know that if she did it once to be with you, there's the possibility that she might get brave and try it again. I want you to know that if that subject ever comes up between you and Denim, I want you to talk her out of it because if she does it, neither one of you will like what happens when I catch you."

With seriousness, Dré looked over at Samuel. "I won't do anything to try and get Denim in trouble, sir."

"I hope you mean that, Dré, because if you two ever try a stunt like that again, you can forget about ever seeing Denim again, and I mean that."

"Yes, sir."

Samuel shook his head in disbelief as he pulled up to a traffic light.

"Son, you teenagers, Denim included, have to realize you can't always have things your way, and you need to learn to use some good judgment."

Dré nodded in agreement. "Mr. Samuel, I know where you're coming from."

"Do you? What about sex? Have you and Denim—"

Cutting him off before he could finish, Dré replied firmly, "No, sir!"

"You wouldn't lie to me, would you?"

Dré squirmed in his seat. He'd definitely dreamed about being with Denim, but he wouldn't dare tell her father. "Mr. Samuel, I've never touched Denim in that way."

Clearing his throat, Samuel gripped the steering wheel. Just the thought of them together made him angry. When the light turned green, Samuel continued to drive while Dré looked out the window in silence.

"I'm really torn right now, Dré. I don't want to shelter Denim too much, but on the other hand, it's my job to protect her. One thing I have to make sure of is that you and Denim understand that when we allow you to take her out, both of you are responsible for abiding by our rules."

"I wouldn't want it any other way, Mr. Samuel. I want you guys to be able to trust me and know that Denim is in good hands when she's with me."

"I honestly believe that you are a decent young man with an amazing future. Don't throw it away by making stupid mistakes."

Dré smiled. "I won't, sir, because I want to get out of Freedman and make something of myself."

"You can do whatever you set your mind to, Dré. Stay away from drugs and crime and keep your grades up, and your dreams will come true, and they'll take you far in life. You're a great athlete, and your artistic skills are remarkable, so don't throw it away."

"Thanks, Mr. Samuel."

Pulling into the parking lot of the auto supply store, Samuel put his car in park and turned to Dré. "You're welcome. Listen, I'm going to let you take Denim to the football game on Friday, but remember her curfew and everything we talked about this evening. Don't let me down."

A huge smile appeared on Dré's face. "Thank you, Mr. Samuel. You don't have to worry about a thing. I'll take good care of Denim."

Opening his car door, Samuel got out. Dré also got out of the car and joined him.

Samuel put his hand on Dré's shoulder. "Son, all I ask is that you treat my daughter like you would want your own daughter treated. If you do that, we'll get along just fine. Okay?"

"Yes, sir," Dré answered as they walked into the auto supply store.

Feeling a little relieved over his conversation with Dré, Samuel clapped his hands together.

"Now, with that out of the way, I need to pick up a few things for Denim's car, so come on so I can teach you a little something about cars."

Dré grabbed a shopping basket and followed Samuel around in the store.

Friday rolled around and the stadium was packed to capacity. It was also cooler than normal, so Denim wore her jacket and also took a blanket. After eating a corn dog, Denim asked Dré to get her some hot chocolate to warm her up. Dré and DeMario left Patrice and Denim in their seats. As soon as they were out of hearing distance, Patrice bumped shoulders with her.

"So, what are you and Dré up to tonight?"

Denim shrugged her shoulders. "Nothing, Patrice. Why do you ask?"

Smiling, Patrice put a nacho chip covered with cheese into her mouth. "That's not what DeMario said."

This got Denim's attention, so she turned to Patrice. "And just what did DeMario tell you?"

"Oops! My bad! Forget I said anything."

Denim yanked the tray of nachos out of her hand. "Tell me, Patrice!" Denim pleaded.

Giggling, Patrice reached over and retrieved her food. "Chill! DeMario wouldn't tell me the details. He just said that Dré had something very special planned for the two of you after the ball game."

Denim noticed the guys on their way back to their seats. She pulled her blanket over her lap.

"Well, whatever it is, Dré knows I have to be home by twelve, so it can't be all that."

Dancing in her seat, Patrice started singing. "It only takes a minute, girl, to fall in love . . . to fall in love."

Denim pushed Patrice playfully. "You're so crazy. Shhhh, here they come."

Dré and DeMario rejoined the girls. Dré handed Denim the cup of hot cocoa and sat down beside her.

"Here's some cocoa for *my* Cocoa Princess."

"Thank you, Prime Time."

Dré slid back under the blanket with Denim and

rested his hand lovingly on her thigh. Denim felt that familiar fluttering in her stomach and tried her best to play it cool, but her insides were going crazy as she sat wondering what plans Dré had for them after the game. She realized she would just have to wait and see.

An hour or so later, the horn sounded, signaling the end of the football game. Freedman High won by two touchdowns, and to celebrate, a party was being held at a local teen club. Dré held Denim's hand as they walked back to his car. On their way, they stopped to chat with some of their classmates. When they reached the car, he turned to Denim.

"Do you want to go grab something to eat?" he asked.

"Sure. I'm sorry I can't go to the party, but if you want to go, you can drop me off at home."

"Nah, I'm cool. After I take you home, I'm going to head home myself," Dré replied as he opened the car door for her.

As Dré drove through town and passed by most of the fast food restaurants, Denim looked out the window curiously.

"Where are we going?" Denim asked. "I thought we were going to get something to eat."

"We are, but at a special spot, just for us," he said with pride. "Don't worry; you're going to love it."

Minutes later, Dré pulled up to an area lake and parked.

"What are we doing out here?" Denim asked nervously.

Without responding, he climbed out of his car and opened up the trunk. He pulled out a wicker basket and a couple of blankets. He came around to the passenger side of the car and opened the door for Denim.

"Come on, Cocoa Princess. We don't have all night."

Denim nervously climbed out of the car. "Dré why are we at the lake?"

He closed the door behind her and said, "So we can have some privacy."

Demin folded her arms around her chest. "It's cold out here."

"Relax, sweetheart. I'll have you all warmed up in just a second," he said, grinning mischievously.

Dré found a grassy area and set the wicker basket down. Next, he took one of the blankets and spread it out for them to sit on.

"Come over here, Denim."

He took her hand and they sat down on the blanket. He opened the basket and pulled out a thermos filled with more hot cocoa. He poured her a cup and pulled her into his lap. He wrapped the other blanket around their shoulders for extra warmth.

Impressed, Denim took a sip of her cocoa and turned to him.

"You never cease to amaze me, Prime Time. Where did you get this cocoa?"

He hugged her tightly. "A friend of mine in the concession stand took care of it for me right before we left the game. I hope you approve, Cocoa Princess."

"I do. What else do you have in that basket?"

He leaned over and opened the basket.

"I have two hamburgers and some fries. I also have another thermos full of hot cocoa in case we need it."

Denim could only smile as she leaned back against his chest. The hot cocoa did warm her, but not as much as sitting in his arms did. They finished their cocoa and looked out over the lake. They could see the reflection of the moon in the water and could hear the sounds of nature all around them.

"It's so beautiful and quiet out here, Dré. You picked a great spot. I could live somewhere like this."

He caressed her cheek and said, "Yeah, I come out here a lot. You can really get your thoughts together out here. I have some nice sketches of this view. I'll show them to you one day."

Denim smiled and kissed Dré on the cheek. That one subtle gesture caused Dré to cup her face and kiss her firmly on the lips. At the lake, there was no audience, no distractions, and no interruptions. She was his Cocoa Princess, and he would love her forever.

They kissed and they kissed. Dré rolled over until his body was on top of hers. It felt sinful yet electrifying as the couple's kisses became even more heated and Dré's hands began to roam over her body. This went on for several minutes, until a soft sound escaped Denim's throat. It startled her out of her heavenly trance, and as she looked up at him, she smiled.

She nuzzled his neck and whispered, "Dré, I'm sorry."

"About what?" he asked as he kissed her eyelid. "You have no reason to be sorry."

She sat up and said, "We should go. It's getting late."

He rolled over onto his back and rested his head on his hands. "We haven't eaten our burgers yet."

Denim gathered their cups. "I know, but I don't want to chance running into anything that might make me miss my curfew."

Dré picked up on her nervousness, so he stood up and started folding the blanket.

"Look, Denim, if you're ready to leave because things got a little hot between us, just say so. I love you, and I wouldn't do anything to make you uncomfortable."

Looking down at the ground, she ran her foot around the blades of grass.

"It's not you, Dré; it's me. You didn't do anything wrong. I love kissing you. You make me feel things I've never felt before."

"Then what is it?" he asked as he picked up the blankets.

She shoved her hands in her jacket pockets and stuttered out her response.

"Well, it's just that . . . you know it's . . . you make me feel out of control, and it scares me."

He smiled, feeling somewhat relieved. "Really? Denim, you have no reason to be scared."

"But I am!" she yelled. "You cause me to let my guard down when I'm with you, and I don't want to get my heart broken," she whispered.

Dré hugged her tightly. "Baby, I'd never break your heart, and when we do finally hook up, I guarantee you it's going to be worth the wait and beyond your wildest dreams. That I promise."

Denim tried to swallow the lump in her throat. Dré had given her a peek of the sensual tryst yet to come between them.

Burying her face against his chest, she did everything she could to keep the tears from running down her cheeks. "I want to be closer to you. I'm just a little nervous about everything. You feel me?"

"You're my girl, Denim, and I love you no matter what, so relax, baby. We're cool. I love you, and nothing will happen between us until you're ready."

"Thank you, Dré. That means a lot to me," she said, relieved.

They stood there in each other's arms in silence as he lovingly caressed her back.

"Come on, Cocoa Princess. Let me get you home."

"Thanks again for the picnic," Denim said as she took the blankets out of Dré's hands. "This was nice before I ruined everything."

"You didn't ruin anything," he said with a smile as he picked up the wicker basket. "We got a chance to talk about something very important between us. I want you to be up front with me anytime something's bothering you. Okay?"

"Okay. We'd better get going. I'm going to eat my burger in the car."

Dré opened the trunk and put the blanket inside. "Me too," he said as he opened her door, allowing her to ease into her seat.

Denim buckled her seatbelt and unwrapped one of the burgers. She held it up to Dré's mouth so he could take a bite while the car warmed up.

"Dang, this is good! My boy at the concession stand really hooked me up."

Denim giggled and took a bite of the sandwich. "Mmmm, you're right. This is delicious!"

Dré buckled his seatbelt and turned the heat up.

"You're beautiful, Denim. I haven't told you tonight, and I didn't want our date to end without me telling you so."

Denim was overwhelmed, but couldn't help remembering her mother's words: *Boys will tell you anything to get you to have sex with them.*

The difference was that Dré wasn't pressuring her. She was the one who wanted to get closer to him. She was just a little nervous . . . for now.

"Thanks, Dré. You look handsome tonight yourself."

He smiled. "Thanks. Now, may I have another bite?" he asked.

"Of course you can," Denim replied as she held the burger up to Dré's mouth. Two bites later, it was gone.

It didn't take long for the car heat up, but before pulling off, Dré decided to produce a little more heat of his own. He leaned over and kissed Denim over and over. She happily accepted his love and affection as she linked her arms around his neck.

Several minutes later, he released her and looked her directly in the eyes. "I love you, Denim Mitchell, and that's not a line. I mean it, and don't you ever forget it."

She kissed him once more and replied, "I won't, and I love you too, André Patterson."

Chapter Twelve

A few weeks later, basketball season kicked off in full swing, and Denim was ready to shake her purple-and-gold pompoms for Dré. Each week, the young couple had gotten closer to each other, but had yet to reach that final plateau of ecstasy they both longed for. Denim was still working at the hospital every weekend, and had actually gotten closer to a lot of the patients and staff in doing so. She did miss sleeping in on Saturday mornings, but when she came home, she was still able to go out with Dré when he got off work.

At the opening basketball game, as expected, Dré was on his way to being the high scorer and rebounder of the game, which was a repeat from last year. College scouts from all over the country were taking notice of his athletic abilities, and it was inevitable that Dré would get an athletic scholarship. The question was, from where?

During halftime, Denim took her break, sitting in the bleachers with Patrice and a few other friends. She sipped on a bottle of Gatorade and nibbled on a hotdog as the band and halftime dancers entertained the crowd.

"So, Denim, how does it feel to finally wear the purple and gold and cheer for Dré?"

Denim giggled and danced to the music. "I cheered for Dré even before I made the cheerleading squad. You know that."

"This is different, sis. You're in uniform and you're out on the floor with him. I see him looking over at you when he runs down the floor."

Denim waved Patrice off. "Girl, Dré is not thinking about me when he's in the game. You know how serious he is when he's playing ball."

Patrice turned her soda cup up and crunched on the ice. "Believe what you want, Denim, but he's definitely checking you out."

Denim shook her head in disbelief.

They enjoyed the halftime show, and when it was over, the team returned to the floor to warm up. Denim watched as Dré did layups and shot several three-point shots. He glanced over at Denim and smiled.

"See, Denim? I told you he was checking you out."

Denim smiled back at Dré. Just making eye contact with him made her neck heat up.

Minutes later, the horn sounded to alert everyone of the beginning of the third quarter. Denim stood and smoothed out her purple skirt. "Well, it's been fun, Patrice, but I have to get back to work."

"Go do your thang, girlfriend!" Patrice yelled. "Woo! Woo!"

Denim looked over at Patrice and laughed. "Do you always have to be so loud?"

"Yes! You look good in your cheerleader uniform. You should get your navel pierced."

Denim walked down a few steps and laughed. "My parents won't let that happen. I'll have to wait until I'm eighteen."

"By then, you probably won't have that flat stomach," Patrice joked.

"I see you have jokes."

"By the way, what are you guys doing after the game?" Patrice asked.

"We'll probably grab something to eat and then hang out at my house for awhile. What about you?"

Patrice winked at Denim mischievously. "You know how me and DeMario roll."

Denim jumped down to the floor and rolled her eyes. "Don't remind me. Y'all really need to give it a rest."

"Don't hate!" Patrice yelled back at Denim as she gave a girl sitting next to her a high five.

Denim returned to her spot on the sidelines to cheer for the team. The basketball game resumed, and approximately an hour later, Freedman High came out as the winner. Denim and all the other cheerleaders ran out on the floor to congratulate the players and to celebrate. As soon as Dré could get close to Denim, he gave her a hug, picking her up off the floor.

With her arms wrapped around his neck, she said, "Good game, Prime Time."

He released her and gave her a quick kiss. "Congratulate me later. I need to shower. You are still riding with me, aren't you?"

She smiled. "Of course I am. I'll wait for you out here."

"I won't be long," he announced.

As he walked toward the locker room, a reporter stopped him for an interview. After a few minutes, he made his way into the locker room with the rest of his teammates.

While waiting for Dré, Denim talked to friends and gathered her duffle bag with her pompoms and other belongings. She sat on the bleachers and called her parents.

"Hello?" Valessa answered.

"Hey, Mom. We won!"

"That's great. Are you still at school?"

Denim waved at some classmates who were walking past. "Yes, ma'am. I'm waiting on Dré to come out of the locker room. We're going to get something to eat and then I'll be home."

"Okay, and tell Dré to drive carefully."

Denim opened another bottle of Gatorade and took a sip. Her mouth felt exceptionally dry. "I will, Mom."

"Okay. Just stick your head in when you get home. Your father's watching TV in the family room. I love you."

"I love you too, Mom."

Denim hung up the telephone and tucked it inside her gold letterman's jacket. Patrice and DeMario walked over and sat down next to her.

"What's up, Denim!" he yelled as he hugged her.

She returned the hug. "Hey, DeMario."

"Are you waiting on your boy?" he asked.

Denim crossed her legs and twirled her finger around a strand of her hair. "You know I am."

"Well, all I have to say is LeBron James had better watch his back because Dré is on the road to breaking every record he ever set!" DeMario yelled as he mimicked some dribbling moves.

"I know that's right!" Patrice agreed loudly as she gave him her signature high five.

Annoyed, Denim turned to them and said, "Don't you guys have somewhere you want to be?"

DeMario put his hand over his heart playfully. "You hurt me, Denim. I thought I was your boy."

She stood up and said, "You are, DeMario. Look, I'm sorry. I guess I'm just tired and ready to go home."

"That's cool, Denim. I feel you," DeMario replied.

Just then, Dré walked out of the locker room with his duffle bag on his shoulder, dressed in a navy blue suit. Denim trembled at the mere sight of him. He looked like Michael Jordan in his suit; he was gorgeous. Dré made his way over to the group and set his duffle bag on the bleachers.

DeMario shook his hand and hugged him. "Dré, I have to give it to you. You killed them tonight."

Without taking his eyes off Denim, he replied, "Thanks, man. Denim, are you ready to go?"

Denim opened her mouth to answer him, but nothing came out. Patrice giggled at seeing Denim all choked up.

Denim cleared her throat and finally said, "Yeah, I'm ready."

Dré hugged Patrice and then picked up Denim's duffle bag. "Let's roll, babe."

All four of them walked toward the exit. DeMario turned to Dré and asked, "Where are you guys headed?"

"What's with all the questions, Oprah?" Dré joked. "Don't you and Patrice already have plans?"

Patrice linked her arm with DeMario's. "Since you ask, Mr. Basketball, we do."

Dré put his arm around Denim's waist and held her close. "Then I guess we'll see you guys tomorrow."

DeMario taped his fist with Dré's. "On that note, we'll holler. Take it easy."

"Good-bye you two," Denim called out to them once they reached the parking lot.

He leaned over and whispered, "You did great tonight."

She looked up at him and asked, "How would you know?"

"I saw you. You have the best looking legs on the squad. How could I miss you?"

Dré opened the car door for Denim so she could slide inside. He put their duffle bags on the backseat and joined her inside the car. He turned on the engine and looked over at her and asked, "Hungry?"

Denim looked him in his eyes and said softly, "A little bit. We could pick up something to eat on the way to your house."

"My house?" he asked as he studied her expression.

Denim reached over, cupped his face, and kissed him hard on the lips. She released him and looked into his eyes before kissing him again. Dré smiled. He knew exactly what Denim was insinuating.

"Are you sure about this?"

"I'm sure. Are your parents still in Vegas?" she asked.

Dré gently caressed her cheek. "Yeah. They won't be back until Sunday."

"Perfect. Just make sure you get me home by my curfew," she reminded him.

Without hesitating, Dré put the car in drive.

On this night, the pair confirmed their love for each other in the most intimate way. For Denim, it was nothing like she ever expected. There was definitely pain, which overshadowed much of the pleasure she had dreamed about. Dré, compassionate about her discomfort, did everything within his power to make sure her first experience was as pleasurable and memorable as possible.

"Are you okay?" he asked.

"I will be," she replied with her voice somewhat strained.

"Do you want me to stop?"

She hugged him tighter and buried her face into his warm neck and whispered. "No, don't stop."

Hearing the confirmation he needed, Dré moved in a slow but precise motion. He could feel Denim's fingernails clawing at his back and hear her sighs of passion. Being as gentle as possible, he was eventually successful in his efforts to comfort her.

Loving Denim was easy, but Dré never thought his love for her would overwhelm him the way it did. Not only were Denim's eyes full of tears, but so were his. Seconds later, Denim's tears were replaced with a smile and sighs of gratification while Dré struggled to maintain control of his emotions. Their bodies joined together as one and heat consumed them with an explosive climax that left both of them sobbing with satisfaction.

They never did get a chance to eat because they spent their remaining time kissing and holding each other. Later that night, Dré drove Denim home and gave her a soul-stirring kiss good night before walking her to the door.

Once inside the house, Denim greeted her father before she retreated to the confines of her room. She lay across her bed and reminisced about her evening with Dré. She opened the drawer on her nightstand pulled out her journal.

Tonight was nothing short of magical. Dré and I made our love official tonight, and I've never felt as close to him as I do right now. Dang! I don't

*know where to start. Loving him was nothing like
I thought it would be. It was painful at first, but
after a few of his kisses, all I could feel was passion from the only man I'll ever love.*

*Dré never made me feel pressured to do ANY-
THING, and making love to him was something I
know I can never do with anyone else. I know he
loves me, and he knows how much I love him too.
It felt natural to feel his warm skin against mine,
but I have to admit that I did get a little nervous
at the last minute when images of Mom and
Daddy popped in my head. Being the sweetheart
Dré is, he assured me everything would be OK,
and he was right. I know without a doubt that I
will love him forever.*

Later,
D

After putting her journal away she felt like screaming
at the top of her lungs. She could still feel Dré's hands
and lips all over her body, and it caused her skin to tin-
gle. She felt her body shivering, and all she wanted to
do was close her eyes and imagine that Dré was lying
right next to her.

"Denim? Are you okay?" Valessa asked.

Startled out of her trance, Denim opened her eyes
and quickly sat up on the side of her bed. "Yes, ma'am."

"I called you three times," Valessa revealed. She
frowned as she walked closer to Denim.

Denim nervously picked up a stuffed bear and held it

149

in her lap protectively. She hoped it would shield her from any evidence of her night with Dré.

"I guess I dozed off," Denim suggested.

Her mother studied her curiously before speaking. "I just wanted to tell you good night. Your father told me you were home. You forgot to stick your head in my room."

"I'm sorry. I figured you were asleep."

Valessa looked around the room and back at Denim. Something didn't feel right, but she couldn't put her finger on it. As she turned to walk out of the room, she said, "Well, hurry up and get your shower so you can go to bed. And don't forget to put your cheerleader uniform in the cleaners tomorrow."

Denim hugged the stuffed bear even tighter and said, "I won't. Good night."

Once her mother was out of the room, she lay back on the bed and sighed. She was afraid her mother had picked up Dré's scent on her body. She had hoped to enjoy his fragrance a little while longer, but decided she'd better go ahead and shower. She put the teddy bear back in place on her bed and grabbed her pajamas and disappeared into the bathroom.

Dré and Denim decided to keep the milestone in their relationship to themselves. One reason was because Patrice had a big mouth, and DeMario wasn't any different. The last thing they wanted was to have their business spread all over school and for their parents to find out. Unfortunately, their love for each other was obvious to everyone who knew them, making it hard for them to hide their secret. Their friends noticed the way the couple looked into each other's eyes, couldn't seem to keep their hands off each other, and lastly, how they spent every spare moment together. It was true love and everyone knew it, even their parents.

Chapter Thirteen

By the time Christmas rolled around, Denim was glowing. Antoine was home, and she'd never been happier. This was Antonie's first trip home from college since May.

One afternoon while their parents were out Christmas shopping, Denim and Antoine got an opportunity to talk privately and catch up on each other's lives. Antoine noticed a difference in his baby sister—physically, emotionally, and mentally.

As they talked, he discovered that Denim had matured and lost her innocence with Dré, and had been hooking up with him on a regular basis. A sickening feeling settled in the pit of his stomach, but it quickly subsided as he remembered his own journey down that path.

He cut two slices of rum cake and sat down at the bar with Denim. He looked over at her and smiled.

"You two *are* taking precautions, aren't you?"

"Yeah, Antoine!" she replied, somewhat embarrassed.

"So, you're cool with everything?" he asked.

"Oh, yes, Antoine. I mean, it was weird at first, but I wanted to be with him so much. I love Dré, and he loves me."

"Why was it so important to you to do it now, Denim? Couldn't you have waited a little longer?"

She put a small piece of cake into her mouth and shrugged her shoulders. "I suppose we could have, but I didn't want to." She closed her eyes and said, "Dré makes me feel unbelievable. It feels so natural being with him."

Antoine shook his head, clearly agitated by Denim's comment, and bit into his slice of cake. He wasn't emotionally prepared to listen to tales of his sister's sexual escapades just yet. To try to diminish the hoopla surrounding her relationship, he said, "Denim, I can guarantee you that while you may feel like you're all in love with Dré now, it'll change. Most people feel like that with their first love. He won't be your last; believe me."

Denim frowned, put her fork down, and turned to her brother. "Don't say that. I could never love another guy like I love Dré."

Antoine took a sip of milk and wiped the milk mustache off his face with his sleeve. "If you say so, sis. Just don't put all your emotions into your first relationship because you're setting yourself up to possibly get hurt. You're still young, and you have a lot of years ahead of you."

She listened to Antoine, but she didn't believe him because all she knew was that Dré was the love of her life, and he would always be the love of her life, regardless of what Antoine or anyone said.

Denim and Dré dated hot and heavy through the holidays. For Christmas, Denim gave Dré an expensive watch and he gave her a heart-shaped locket with a picture they'd taken in a photo booth. Denim couldn't ask for a better gift; it kept Dré close to her heart at all times.

Work at the hospital was still going well, and in January, Denim started rotating between the rehab center and the children's ward. This gave her the opportunity to make even more friends, especially with the children who suffered from some severe illness. Life was good, and being in love with Dré and working with her patients was what kept Denim going.

Then, the weekend before Valentine's Day, her life unexpectedly came to a screeching halt. Dré and his entire family had mysteriously moved out of their house and disappeared. No one knew where the family had gone, and no one had seen them move out of the house. All they knew was that the house was empty.

Denim tried calling Dré's cell phone, but it was disconnected. Frantic, she called DeMario.

"DeMario! Have you seen or talked to Dré?" she yelled into the telephone.

"Calm down, Denim. No, I haven't seen Dré since yesterday. Why?"

Denim was sobbing now. "Because he's missing. His whole family is gone. Their house is empty, and he's not answering his cell phone."

DeMario climbed out of bed and said, "What are you talking about? I'm supposed to meet Dré later today to play ball."

"Where could he be, DeMario?" she asked with her voice cracking.

"I don't know, Denim. The last time I saw him was yesterday. Look, I'll see if I can find him and get back to you, okay? Don't worry; I'll find him."

Denim thanked DeMario and hung up the telephone. Her heart was racing and she felt faint. As she sat there, she prayed that Dré hadn't abandoned her and the love they had between them.

Unfortunately, neither DeMario nor Samuel could find out any information on the Pattersons or their whereabouts. Samuel walked into Denim's room and sat on the side of her bed.

"I'm sorry, Denim, but no one knows anything. I've asked around, but I can't find one person who has any information on Dré and his parents. Don't worry; I'm sure Dré will contact you soon and let you know where he is and why they moved so suddenly."

Denim hugged her pillow and asked, "Can't we call the police?"

"It's not a crime for people to move out of their house, sweetheart. Just give it time. I'm sure Dré will call," her father assured her before walking out of her room.

Denim felt queasy and needed to throw up. She put her hand over her mouth and ran to the bathroom and held her head over the porcelain bowl, sick and heartbroken.

Hours passed, and sadly, Dré didn't call, leaving Denim unable to sleep or eat. She was devastated and felt betrayed because Dré had broken the first promise he made to her, which was to never let her down. The burning question inside her was why he left and why he hadn't called, emailed, or texted her. It was as if he had vanished off the face of the earth.

The next day, Denim walked down the street and took one last look at Dré's house and then cried the entire way home. She felt as though a dark cloud was hovering over her head, shadowing all the happiness and sunshine she ever had. Once inside the confines of her room, she opened her nightstand and pulled out her journal.

Life is not fair, and love is definitely overrated. My world has come to a complete stop. Dré and his family are gone, and I don't feel like I'll ever be able to breathe again. God, I need answers and I need Dré. Where is he, and how could he leave me without saying a word?

Later,
D

A week later, there was still no word from Dré, and Denim's heart was crushed beyond anyone's imagination. She tried to use the Internet to locate the Pattersons, but was unsuccessful. Denim had no choice but to throw herself into school and her job. She needed something to concentrate on to keep her mind off Dré. Unfortunately, all school did was remind her of Dré. People kept coming up to her, asking her where he had moved to and why he had moved. Unable to give them a legitimate answer, she retaliated in anger and put a wall up between her and her classmates.

Dré's mysterious and sudden departure had taken a toll on Denim emotionally, and she had become a work-aholic. Luckily, through her determination and success-ful relationship with her patients, she was offered a position as a regular employee, with pay. Her parents re-luctantly allowed her to increase her schedule to work a few hours after school, as well as every weekend. With Dré gone, her evenings and weekends were insignificant, so she thought she might as well make some money.

Denim loved her job. She assisted the physical thera-pist in the rehab clinic in the hospital. While she was going through her own hell full of emotional pain, what she witnessed her patients going through was far worse than her misery.

Things got even worse when Patrice got pregnant, which made their pact of going off to college together nothing but a distant memory. This made Denim angry, and she selfishly stopped associating with Patrice alto-gether.

One day, while Denim was cleaning her room, the doorbell rang. She answered it and found Patrice stand-ing on her porch.

"What are you doing here?" Denim asked sarcasti-cally.

Patrice took a breath and asked, "May I come in? We need to talk."

Denim stepped back and said, "About what?"

Patrice walked into the house and followed Denim up to her room. Once inside Denim's room, she turned and asked, "Why won't you return my calls, Denim?"

Denim sat down on the side of her bed and folded her arms. "Because you're stupid! How could you go off and get yourself pregnant?"

Patrice put her hands on her stomach and said, "I didn't plan it, Denim, but I want this baby. DeMario loves me just as much as Dré loved you."

Denim jumped off her bed and put her finger in Patrice's face. "Leave Dré out of it! This has nothing to do with him."

Patrice frowned and said, "You're just jealous, Denim."

"Why would I be jealous? You're the one who's going to be tied down with a baby and not get to go to college like we planned!"

Patrice wiped some stray tears off her cheeks and said, "Is that what this is all about? Do you ever think about anybody else besides yourself? I thought you were my friend. I thought you would be happy for me."

"How could I be happy for you when you've ruined your life?" Denim spat back at her.

"How can being a mother ruin my life? Besides, it's my life! I'm happy! Maybe if you would get off your butt and stop feeling sorry for yourself, you could be happy too."

Denim walked over to her door, opened it, and angrily yelled, "Get out of my house!"

Patrice walked toward the door and said, "Fine! If that's the way you want it, you don't ever have to worry about me bothering you again. Have a nice life . . . friend."

Denim slammed her door and fell across her bed in tears. From that day forward, the girls who'd been friends since third grade grew apart.

The argument with Patrice didn't help Denim's demeanor. She was angry all the time and had become anti-social except when she was at the hospital. Normalcy was what her parents wanted for their daughter, but their household was nowhere near normal. They had no idea that Denim's feelings for Dré were so strong, and they were extremely worried about her.

Dré had been gone for weeks now, and the numbness of his absence was starting to wear off. Denim was still heartbroken, but she'd begun to slowly open up to the outside world. One night, after doing her homework, checking her emails and surfing the Internet for a while, Denim showered and got ready for bed. By the time she pulled back the comforter on her bed, it was nearly midnight. At that time, her cell phone rang. Not wanting it to wake her parents, she quickly answered. "Hello?"

There was silence on the other end of the telephone. Denim sat down on the side of the bed. "Hello? Is anybody there?"

Once again, silence. Then as if a light bulb went off in her head, she whispered, "Dré?"

At that moment, she heard a click. The line went dead, and she nervously checked her inbound call log. The number came up UNKNOWN on the display. *Could it have been Dré?* The last thing she wanted to do was to get her hopes up.

That night, sleep didn't come easy to her, but she was finally able to drift off into a deep slumber. She prayed that if it was Dré, he would call her back again.

The next morning, as Denim retrieved her textbooks out of her locker, Anika and a couple of her friends walked over to her. Anika leaned again the locker and said, "Looks like somebody can't keep a man. Even he couldn't stand to be around you, so he moved."

Without saying a word, Denim slammed her locker closed and hit Anika so hard in the nose, she knocked her feet away from under her. Anika hit the floor hard, and blood immediately spewed out her nose. "My nose! You broke my nose!"

Demin stood over her and glared down at her. "You got off lucky! You need to think twice before coming anywhere near me again."

Anika's friends helped her off the floor as Denim made her way down the hall and around the corner to her next class; however, she wasn't there long. While Anika spent the next thirty minutes in the nurse's office, Denim was summoned to the principal's office. It took him all of fifteen minutes to hand her a two-day suspension for fighting.

"Denim, I don't know what has gotten into you. You've never been in trouble like this before. You're lucky Anika wasn't seriously injured and that you've always been a model student. Otherwise, I would have to expel you. Your teachers said you're in class physically, but your mind is somewhere else. Is there something going on that I need to know about?"

Denim stood. "No, sir."

"Then get it together before you mess up your academic career. Now, I've called your mother and told her what happened. You can finish the rest of the day, but I hope you use the next two days to reevaluate what happened and return to school with a better attitude."

"Yes, sir," she replied as she turned and walked out the door.

As soon as Denim arrived home, her mother met her at the door. "Fighting? Denim, this has got to stop. I know you've been unhappy since Dré disappeared, but you'd better get it together, young lady."

Denim threw her books on the floor. "Mom I was just defending myself! Don't you want to hear my side of the story?"

"I know you're not raising your voice to me! There are other ways to handle disagreements outside of fighting," Valessa yelled back. She pointed to the stairs. "Go to your room before you make me hurt you!"

Denim picked up her books and yelled, "Fine! I'm already hurt, so there's not much more you could do to me."

Valessa stood there in shock at her daughter's behavior. She watched her as she stomped her way up to her room and slammed her bedroom door closed, shaking the entire house.

"Oh, hell no," Valessa mumbled as she headed for the stairs just as Samuel walked through the door. He noticed the stress in her face.

"What's all that noise in here?"

Valessa walked over to the kitchen table and sat down. "Samuel, Denim got suspended from school for fighting. She broke a girl's nose."

Samuel set his keys on the countertop and frowned. "Denim was fighting? What happened?"

"I never got a chance to ask her. She came in here acting like a militant, throwing her books on the floor and yelling. I know she's upset about Dré's disappearance, but this has got to stop before she makes me kill her."

Samuel took a breath and walked toward the stairs. "I'll talk to her."

Upstairs, Denim wrote vigorously in her journal:

I finally put Anika in her place today. I hope her nose grows back crooked. I HATE HER! Being suspended for two days won't be so bad. At this point, I don't care. Mom is pissed and I know she can't wait to tell Daddy when he comes home.

Sometimes I wish I could just quit school and work at the hospital full time. Since Dré left, I'm happiest when I'm with my patients.

On Sunday, Pastor said God has a plan for everyone. What is my plan? I need to know because I feel so lost. There are times I wish that I was like Patrice. What if I was pregnant with Dré's child? At least I would have a part of him still with me, but I would still be alone. Dré! Where are you???

A knock on the door interrupted her. "Denim, it's your father."

Denim put her journal back into her nightstand and walked across the room to open her door. As soon as she made eye contact with him, she knew why he was there.

He walked through the door and sat down in her chair. "Sit down, sweetheart. I want to talk to you."

She sat down and waited for her father's wrath. Instead, she got the opposite. "What happened at school today?"

Denim swallowed hard and closed her eyes briefly. "This girl named Anika cornered me at my locker and blamed me for Dré's disappearance."

"What gave her that idea?" Samuel asked.

Denim ran her hands through her hair and tears welled up in her eyes. "She never liked me, Daddy, and she never like the fact that I was going out with Dré. She's mean and I hate her!"

"So, you've had problems with her before?"

"Yes, but today got the best of me, and I guess I snapped."

Samuel thought for a moment. "Are you saying you were defending yourself?"

"I guess. I tried to tell Mom, but she wouldn't listen."

Samuel sighed. "It doesn't matter. Your mother said you were being defiant the moment you walked into the house."

Denim lowered her head with guilt. Samuel covered his eyes with his hands for a moment.

"Denim, life goes on. Love is going to come and go many times in your lifetime. There had to be a legitimate reason for Dré and his family to leave like they did, but you can't keep holding on to all this bitterness. I'm sure one day you'll hear from him and he'll be able to explain everything to you. In the meantime, your mother and I want you to get your act together. All we ask you to do is keep you grades up, focus on your job, and try to get past your pain over Dré. Can you work on that for us, please?"

Tears dropped out of Denim's eyes. She looked at her father and said, "I'm trying, Daddy."

He stood and said, "Then try harder. While you're on suspension, call your supervisor and let her know you're able to work full time the next two days. Also, make sure you get your class assignments so you won't get behind in your work, and lastly, go apologize to your mother—and I don't ever want to hear about you disrespecting her again. Do you understand me?"

"Yes, sir."

He walked over and pulled her into his arms. "You're forgiven. Now, I hope to see the daughter I had a few weeks ago at dinner. Okay?"

Denim nodded without responding.

Chapter Fourteen

At the hospital, Denim arrived early to get her patient assignment. Since she'd been working in the physical therapy department, Denim had decided to major in it when she got to college. After logging her start time in on the computer, she picked up her file and walked into the fitness room. Jason, the physical therapist who had trained her, was working with a patient. He looked up and greeted her cheerfully.

"Good Morning, Denim. What a surprise. Why aren't you at school?"

She walked over to him and sat down on a Pilates ball. "You don't want to know."

Jason laughed. "I think I do. Okay, Miss Gladys, give me ten more leg lifts."

Jason assisted his patient, who was recovering from hip replacement surgery. As she did her routine, Jason counted off the leg lifts. "I'm waiting, Denim. Why are you here on a school day?"

She giggled. "I got in a fight at school and I'm suspended for two days."

Jason laughed out loud. "That's hard to believe. You're so sweet."

Quoting from the ad of a beer commercial, she stood and joked, "Don't let the smooth taste fool you."

Jason shook his head in disbelief at Denim. "Okay, Miss Gladys. You're done with your leg lifts. Now I'm going to put you on the treadmill for ten minutes, and this time, do not change the speed. Agreed?"

Miss Gladys, a sixty-year-old widow, winked at Jason and followed him over the treadmill. After he got her started, he walked back over to Denim and took the file out of her hand.

As he scanned the file, he asked, "Did your fight have anything to do with Dré?"

Denim nodded without answering. Jason was the only person she had confided in about Dré, and he understood her heartache. In fact, Jason had been therapeutic in helping her deal with her anguish.

He handed the file back to Denim and looked her in the eyes. "Let it go, Denim. I promise you, one day you'll look back on it and ask yourself why you wasted so much time feeling sorry for yourself. Life has a way of playing some tricks on you that you might not understand while you're going through them, but in the end, it'll all become clear. Do you understand?"

She wiped away a stray tear and nodded in agreement.

Jason patted her shoulder and said, "Okay, Laila Ali, since you're going to be spending the next two days with me, you'll be working with Mr. Carlton Miller. Here's the scoop: At the moment, he's a paraplegic, but his doctors are optimistic that he will walk again. Do you think you can handle it?"

Feeling much better, Denim clapped her hands together. "Of course I can! So, where is this Carlton Miller?"

"He should be here any minute. Oh, there he is now," Jason pointed out as a nurse wheeled Mr. Miller into the room.

Denim was waiting on a fifty-something, overweight, middle-aged man. What she got was an extremely handsome eighteen-year-old young man with long lashes, warm eyes, and a soft voice.

Jason handed Denim the file and said, "Here you go, Denim. You know what to do."

Denim cleared her throat and said, "Thanks, Jason."

He smiled. "For what?"

"Everything."

"Denim, you are going to be a great P.T. In fact, you already are. That's why I recommended you for the open position. Stop fighting at school and stay on the honor roll so you can get into a good college. You have a bright future in medicine, and I'll do everything within my power to help you succeed.

"Now, get to work. Mr. Miller is waiting on you," Jason said as he walked over to Miss Gladys and got her off the treadmill.

Denim smiled and made her way over to her patient

to begin his treatment. She extended her hand to him and said, "Good morning, Mr. Miller. My name is Denim, and I'll be assisting you with your physical therapy today."

He slowly extended his hand and said, "You can call me Carlton. How old are you?"

Denim smiled and said, "I'm sixteen."

"You're a little young for this job, aren't you?"

With Jason's assistance, she helped him out of the wheelchair and down onto the mat. "Not really. I started out as a volunteer. Now I'm on the payroll."

Jason gave Carlton a playful punch in the arm and said, "Don't worry, Carlton. I'm leaving you in excellent hands."

Carlton smiled and said, "No doubt."

"Carlton, I'm expecting you to behave yourself. Denim's one of our best therapists."

"Word?"

"Word," Jason repeated as he left the two of them alone.

Denim smiled and asked, "So, Carlton, are you ready?"

"As ready as I'm going to be."

"Okay, then let's get this party started," Denim joked.

Carlton laughed. It was obvious that he was smitten with Denim, not only because of her beauty, but because of her abilities as well.

Once the strenuous session was over, Jason helped Denim put Carlton back into his wheelchair. Carlton looked at Jason and said, "Man, you weren't kidding. She tried to kill me."

Jason laughed. "That's a good thing, Carlton. Denim and I will have you back on your feet in little or no time."

Carlton gave Jason a brotherly handshake and said, "That's what I want. Thanks, man."

While the two of them talked, Denim made notes of her session with Carlton in her laptop. "Okay, Carlton, you're good to go. I'll call the nurse to come back and get you."

"If you have the time, I'd rather you take me back to my room."

Surprised, Denim looked over at Jason, who nodded his approval. "Okay, Carlton, let me put my laptop down and we can be on our way."

That night, before going to bed, Denim made an entry in her journal.

Today was a surprisingly wonderful day. My new patient is a cute guy named Carlton Miller. He has the sweetest eyes and the warmest smile. Unfortunately, he's a paraplegic and has a long recovery ahead of him, but I have no doubt he'll make it (with my help, of course). Maybe getting suspended from school wasn't such a bad thang after all. I love helping people, and I'm going to challenge myself to help Carlton and see where life takes me from here.

Later,
D

Days turned in weeks, and weeks into months. Carlton was making tremendous strides in his recovery, and was now using a walker instead of a wheelchair. He'd gotten some feeling back in his legs, and Denim had gotten some feelings back into her heart. On this day, during physical therapy, Denim had Carlton walking between the stationary railings.

He looked over at her and asked, "Denim, is there anyone special in your life?"

"Not really."

He sighed. "I used to have someone special, but she broke up with me after my accident."

"I'm sorry," Denim said softly. "Keep going, Carlton. You're doing great. When you get to the end, turn around and come back toward me."

Carlton did as he was told, putting one foot in front of the other. "What about you?" he asked. "Are you looking for someone special in your life?"

"I don't want to talk about it, Carlton. Just keep walking and think about what you're doing. If you get tired, rest for five seconds, but keep going."

He laughed. "I see I've struck a nerve. What did he do to you?"

Denim put her hands on her hips and said, "Keep your mind on what you're doing."

"I can't. All I can think about is you."

Denim sighed and walked closer to him. She didn't want to admit it, but she had become very attracted to him over the past few months. "That's enough for today. I see you have misbehaving on your mind."

Carlton grabbed his cane and walked over to Denim. "I guess that means I don't have a chance, huh?"

Denim had to admit that Carlton was very good looking, and she'd definitely thought about the possibilities between them, but she couldn't let that cloud her judgment, so she did her best to fight the temptation.

"Carlton, I don't go out with my patients."

He sat down on the bench next to Denim as she typed her notes into the laptop. "That's cool, because I won't be your patient much longer, so I can wait. As a matter of fact, this is my last week with you."

Denim looked over at him and smiled. "You're right. You've been a pain in the butt most of the time, but all in all you've been great patient, Carlton. I'm so happy to see that you're on your way."

He smiled, and Denim hadn't seen a smile so warm in such a long time.

Carlton grabbed his cane and stood. "Will you walk me out, Denim? My mom should be picking me up downstairs any minute."

She set her laptop down and said, "Sure."

Denim escorted Carlton down the hallway and to the elevator. Once outside, the two of them sat on a nearby bench and waited for Carlton's ride.

He looked over to her and asked, "Denim, is the reason you won't give us a chance because of what happened to me, or because I'm not a whole man yet?"

She frowned. "Stop saying that. You are a whole man."

"Then is it because of what happened to me?"

Denim looked at him curiously. "I'm sorry, but I don't know what you're talking about."

Carlton tapped his cane on the sidewalk in silence. "I thought you knew. Isn't it in my file?"

Denim turned to him. "What are you trying to tell me?"

Without answering, he leaned over and kissed her on the lips. Denim froze, unable to pull away. In fact, she deepened the kiss between them, and it felt heavenly. Carlton was a fine man who had her stomach turning flips. It had been so long since she'd felt like kissing any guy, and if it was going to be anybody, she was glad it was Carlton. Dré had left some high standards for the next man in her life to fulfill, and at the moment, Carlton was doing a great job.

Seconds later, Carlton's mother blew her car horn, startling the two of them apart. Embarrassed, Denim jumped off the bench and nervously looked around.

"I'm sorry. I shouldn't have done that."

Carlton put his hand on her cheek and said, "You did what your heart told you to do, and I must say, you taste heavenly, Denim. I hope to get a chance to do it again. I'll see you tomorrow."

Denim felt strange. She watched as Carlton climbed into the car with his mother and drove off. Denim stood there in total shock of her public display of affection, and with a patient, no less. She reached up and touched her lips, which were still tingling from Carlton's sizzling kiss.

"Get a hold of yourself, Denim," she mumbled.

She was somewhat dazed over Carlton's kiss, but was able to regroup before walking back into the hospital. Then, just as she approached the automatic doors, Dré stepped out of the shadows and grabbed her by the shoulders.

He yelled angrily, "Who was that guy kissing you?"

Denim put her hand over her mouth to keep herself from screaming. "Oh my God!"

Chapter Fifteen

"Yeah, it's me. Why were you kissing that guy?" he asked.

Stunned, Denim really didn't know what to say. It was obvious that Dré had seen her kissing Carlton. "It was good-bye kiss."

"Oh, really?" Dré asked, clearly agitated from witnessing Denim and Carlton together.

"Yes, really."

There was silence between the couple for a few seconds. Denim moved closer to Dré. She reached up and touched his face and softly asked, "Dré, where have you been?"

He removed her hands and sat down on the flower bench. "It's not important. What's important is finding out why you would be kissing another man."

Denim's anger overtook her. "How dare you show up

out of the blue and demand answers from me? You left me, remember? I don't owe you an explanation, but you damn sure owe me one."

With tears in his eyes, Dré got up without responding and started walking toward the parking lot.

Denim chased after him and grabbed his arm, stopping him. "Dré, please don't go. That guy was just a patient of mine."

Dré stared at her. She was even more beautiful than he remembered. "Well, from where I was standing, he seems like a lot more than just a patient."

Tears fell from Denim's eyes. She held his hands and asked softly again, "Where have you been? I've been worried sick about you, Dré."

"I've been somewhere missing you," he revealed. "But I can't say where."

"Why not?" she asked. "Don't you think I deserve to know?"

He shook his head. "I just can't."

Denim wrapped her arms around his waist and laid her head against his chest and listened to his heartbeat. "I've missed you so much."

He tilted her chin and then quickly covered her mouth with his. The couple kissed feverishly for a few seconds until Dré broke their kiss. With his voice cracking, he said, "I have to go."

Not wanting to release him, she asked, "Go where, Dré? What or who are you running from?"

He smiled. "I love you, Denim. I can't explain anything to you right now, but I will in due time. I know I don't have a right to be angry at you for kissing that guy, but I am. I never could stand to see another guy looking at you, let alone touch you, so yeah, I'm a little pissed right now, but I'll deal with it."

"It was just a kiss, Dré. It didn't mean anything. What's going on? Why did you and your family leave? Why all the secrecy? Are you in trouble?"

He cleared his throat and said, "It's not what you think, Denim."

"Then explain it to me," she pleaded.

His eyes were full of tears. "That's not important. Have I lost you?"

She lowered her head.

"So much has happened, Dré. It would help if I knew what was going on."

With his voice barely above a whisper, he said, "I can't do that right now. Please tell me I haven't lost you."

Denim wanted so badly to reassure Dré. "I still love you, Dré."

He sighed as if a huge weight had been lifted off his shoulders. He whispered, "Thank God."

"You hurt me, Dré, and I don't know if I can trust you with my heart anymore."

He stepped forward and cupped her face. "I love you, Denim, and that's all you need to know for now."

Denim was desperate for answers. "Dré, please let me help you with whatever it is."

"No!" he replied with an elevated tone. "Just being here could put you in danger."

It was clear to Denim that Dré was in some kind of trouble, and she wished he would let her help him. Before walking off, he gave her one more heated kiss. Then, just as quickly as he had appeared, he was gone.

Epilogue

It had been an exhausting day for Denim, both emotionally and physically. The whole incident seemed like a dream as she drove home in somewhat of a daze. Seeing Dré had shaken her foundation, and if anything, Dré had added more of a mystery to his disappearance.

When Denim pulled into the driveway, she was glad to see that her parents were not home. She wasn't in the mood for a lot of conversation after kissing Carlton and then running into Dré. She entered the house, checked the mail sitting on the counter, and then slowly climbed the stairs. After taking a shower, she climbed into bed and pulled out her journal.

I can't say what I want to say about my day today. What I can say is that it was very interesting, and I'm more confused than I ever was after

Dré disappeared. I was seduced by someone that I've found myself becoming attracted to. It feels weird, and I just pray that in due time, all will reveal itself, so I'll have a better understanding of where my life is supposed to be. I will trust and continue to love, until I know the truth about EVERYTHING.

Later,
D

Denim put her journal back into her nightstand and decided to call it a night. She skipped dinner, turned off the light, and hugged her pillow until she drifted off to sleep.

The next morning, Denim's alarm clock woke her up to prepare her for another day at school. Denim threw back the comforter and turned on the TV. She stood and yawned before making her way into the bathroom. While in the bathroom brushing her teeth, she heard something on the news that caught her attention:

Carlton Miller, a known drug dealer better known as Li'l Carl, was found beaten to death in an alley off Main Street last night. Miller had just recovered from gunshot wounds he'd suffered after a shooting at a birthday party last year that nearly cost him his life. Authorities suspect the murder is the result of an ongoing feud over territory. Police are asking anyone with any infor-

*mation on this crime to call CrimeStoppers im-
mediately.*

The news story really hit home when a picture of
Carlton flashed up the TV screen. Denim got weak in
the knees when reality smacked her in the face. Carlton
Miller, her patient, was the notorious, Li'l Carl, who
was shot at Dré's birthday party.

To be continued
in
Denim Diaries: Grown in 60 Seconds
Coming April 2009